THE PROCESS OF ELIMINATION

An Abaddon Books™ Publication
www.abaddonbooks.com
abaddon@rebellion.co.uk

Published in 2018 by Abaddon Books™,
Rebellion Intellectual Property Limited,
Riverside House, Osney Mead,
Oxford, OX2 0ES, UK.

10 9 8 7 6 5 4 3 2 1

Creative Director and CEO: Jason Kingsley
Chief Technical Officer: Chris Kingsley
Head of Books and Comics Publishing: Ben Smith
Editors: David Thomas Moore,
Michael Rowley and Kate Coe
Marketing and PR: Remy Njambi
Design: Sam Gretton, Oz Osborne and Maz Smith
Cover: Michael Carroll & Pye Parr

Rico Dredd created by
Pat Mills and Mick McMahon.

ISBN: 978-1-78108-037-5

RICO DREDD THE TITAN YEARS

THE PROCESS OF ELIMINATION

MICHAEL CARROLL

ABADDON BOOKS

WWW.ABADDONBOOKS.COM

Prologue

Every prisoner has a mental clock that counts down, slowly eroding the days until release. They might not admit it, but they watch that clock. Constantly. There's always a part of their brain that's aware of how much time they have left to serve.

Except in cases of brain damage or illness or just plain stupidity, no prisoner in the history of the universe has ever been surprised to hear a guard say, "Today's the day. You're outta here. You've done your time."

Sometimes that countdown clock gets nudged back up a little. An extra year for an escape attempt, maybe. Or a couple of days for being involved in a fight. A month for hiding contraband. That kind of thing.

Once in a very long while, the countdown clock gets nudged in the *other* direction.

That happened to me.

It was quite a neat way of doing things, I suppose. Instead of telling the prisoners that you'll add time to their sentence if they don't cooperate—the prisoners might react negatively—you take time away and let them know that it just as easily could be returned. With interest. I saw the same thing when I was a Judge on the streets of Mega-City One: warning a citizen not to do something or she'll go to the cubes is far less effective than telling her that if she *does* do it, her benefits will be cut.

The word around the prison was that I had only barely survived my time out in the Bronze, that the search party had pulled me back from the edge of death. That's close to the truth, anyway. Close, but not all the way there. Someone else had found me.

I still didn't know who, or how. I remember the readouts on my last oxygen tank. The needle steadily dipping toward the red line. I remember thinking that suffocation was probably a better way to go than starvation. And then I fell—again—and that time I didn't even have the strength to rise up against Titan's weak gravity.

So I lay there, lacking the ability to roll onto my back and look up at the stars as I waited for death, until even keeping my eyes open became too much for me.

I was the only one who'd survived the storm, which presented the warden with something of a dilemma. I was a liability—I knew that the prison was *not* the only installation on Titan—but if they brought back nothing but bodies, the inmates might get it into their heads that we'd been found and executed. Letting me live hammered home the futility of an escape attempt. You get where I'm going with this? I *had* to survive, to prove that it wasn't *possible* to survive.

But they couldn't restore me to health and leave me intact. That wouldn't look good at all. It had to be clear that I'd suffered.

Sub-warden Copus said there was some debate as to whether I should lose an arm, or a leg. But I was here to work, he told me.

I don't feel cold any more. I can walk out into the Bronze without an environment suit. No oxygen tanks to carry, no constant fear that the suit will snag on a jagged edge, no more getting to the end of a shift feeling like I've been marinating in my own sweat and urine.

They laced my skin with a tough insulating polymer. Coated my eyes with transparent plastic. Cut out my lungs and fitted me with a biomechanical apparatus that allows me to breathe in Titan's toxic atmosphere. Replaced my vocal cords with an electronic voicebox. Augmented my blood with an artificial fluid, resistant to sub-zero temperatures.

They stripped away my humanity and turned me into a gruddamned monster. A grey, ugly-as-sin cyborg.

But they knocked a year off my sentence.

So, y'know, swings and roundabouts.

Titan
2084 AD

One

It's said that even the toughest prisoner is no match for Titan. *Everyone* breaks, they say.

The cold, the storms, the darkness, the endless labour, the sporadic nocturnal screaming sessions, the ever-present danger from the guards and the other prisoners, the days that last three hundred and eighty-two hours, the constant risk of suffocation in Titan's toxic air, the food so utterly bland that sometimes you'd happily murder everyone on the whole drokkin' moon just for the chance to lick the pot a potato had been boiled in.

Most prisoners broke, eventually; a few didn't. I didn't. Never broke down, never once allowed myself to roll over and expose that emotional underbelly. Displaying a weakness like that in such a hostile environment is the equivalent of handing the other guy a gun and showing him where on your chest you wanted him to aim.

Cadmus Robert Holland—male, Caucasian, fifty-something—finally crumbled, more than a year into his sentence. We'd long since exhausted the pool on him and just taken it as solid that he wasn't going to crack.

We all knew *why* Holland was there, of course, known that from the start. He'd murdered his brother. Bludgeoned him to death with his fists in a frenzy of pure rage. For someone not trained in hand-to-hand combat, that's a pretty impressive feat. Sure, anyone can knock someone over so they hit their head and that kills them, but to actually cave in a human skull using only your knuckles? That takes a special kind of fury.

Otherwise, the only remarkable thing about Cadmus Holland was that he was one of the final batch of Mega-City One citizens sentenced to Titan. Other cities kept sending civilians for the next few years, but someone in the Big Meg had decided that the mining colony on Titan was too harsh a punishment for cits, and fit only for wayward Judges.

It was late November, 2084. A bunch of us had been assigned to cable-duty on J-shaft. Assignments were usually fixed, and most of the time I was outside the prison compound, but sometimes a dig would be picked clean and we'd have to wait until another one was found; or sometimes, the weather was just too bad. That was when they put us on J. It wasn't the worst duty—that would be waste management, and believe me, you do *not* want to know the details—but it was hard work, especially pulley duty.

The shaft was inside the prison compound, and was the primary reason the prison had been built just there. A rich, almost vertical seam of iridium ore that even after all these years still hadn't been exhausted. The yield was about a kilogramme of iridium for every two tonnes we dug out. That might not sound like much, but it gave the average astrogeologist palpitations.

The shaft was a narrow cone, fifty metres across at the surface and three hundred metres deep, with a few small side-tunnels that snaked away, following smaller deposits. It was covered by a sturdy, three-storey-high framework, housing thirty or so mechanical pulley blocks.

That day, former Sov Judge Zera Kurya and I joined eighteen other prisoners hauling on the pulley cables, two prisoners to a cable. We nodded the usual greetings to the teams on either side of us—Cadmus Holland and Artherus Schiller were on our right—and then untied our cables and started to pull.

Arm over arm, steadily hoisting up huge steel buckets of ore. When they reached the pulley block, we switched to a second cable that pulled the bucket forward until it was clear of the pit, then tipped it into the back of a waiting truck.

The trucks took the ore to the smelter, which refined the metal, depositing bars of iridium in neat stacks. Back on Earth, any one of those bars could set someone up for life. Here on Titan, they were just piled up, waiting for the next ship to collect them.

It took an average of four hundred arm-pulls to get a bucket up from the lowest level of the pit. I know: I'd counted. It was exhausting, tedious, back-breaking work and everyone hated it. Most jobs in the prison you'd find someone who didn't mind it, but not this.

New fish always think that they'll be okay with it, and for the first few hours it's not so bad. The buckets weigh about half a tonne fully laden; but with two people lifting, that's only two-hundred and fifty kilogrammes each. And the pulley block has a ten-to-one ratio—for every metre you pull, the bucket is raised ten centimetres—so you're really only lifting twenty-five kilograms. In Titan's low gravity, that's hardly any work at all.

Until you have to do it over and over, a twelve-hour shift, in your bulky, uncomfortable environment suit, on your feet the whole time. You get three twenty-minute breaks per shift, and no talking if certain guards are supervising.

I had it a little easier because mods only do ten-hour shifts when we're working outside: after that, we have to purge our sinus filters, and no one wants to see that.

Six hours into the shift our supervising guard, Delaney, called second break. Delaney was a barrel-chested man with rosy cheeks and white bushy eyebrows. Donny Guildford had once whispered to me that he looked like Santa Claus had gone into witness protection, and that had stuck with me ever since. We liked him; he was one of those guards who wasn't paranoid enough to equate casual conversation with sedition.

As we all gratefully tied off our cables and sat down on the frozen ground, Cadmus Holland said, "I'm done."

Artherus Schiller asked, "You've done what?"

Inside his helmet, Holland slowly shook his head. "I can't go on. This drokkin' place... The air is poison, nothing grows in the frozen dirt, the storms wind can tear you apart. And for what? For *this*." He picked up a small chunk of rock and bounced it in the palm of his hand. "Iridium." He pointed straight up. "There are whole *asteroids* made of the stuff up there. Much closer to home than we are." To Kurya, he said, "I heard your people are talking about setting up a mass-driver in the asteroid belt. Shoot the damn things at Earth, let them burn up in the atmosphere, save the cost of smelting them to get the ore out. That's the way it should be done."

"Probably wasn't their idea," Schiller said. "The Sovs don't invent. They just take other people's ideas. You know? Communism. Even the ideas belong to the state. No offence, Kurya."

"Die in pain," she responded calmly.

I said, "Schiller, shut that down right now. And you can drop the 'I can't take it any more' attitude too, Holland. You can and you will. Your first week, you thought you weren't going to survive, am I right?"

He nodded. "Yeah, but—"

"You were wrong then. Never thought you'd make it through your first month either, or your first year. Same as the rest of us. But you were wrong then too. You *did* make it. Now you think you can't make it to the end of your sentence. What makes you right about that when you were wrong before?"

Schiller gave a half-laugh, half-snort. "Dredd's right. You'll get back to Earth. Start your life over."

Then Holland said, "Without my brother."

"Yeah, well, *you're* the one who caved in his skull. You crack an egg, you can't go complaining that the yolk is leaking out, right?"

Normally, Holland would have either completely ignored that, or responded with a brisk head-butt. This time, he just nodded.

Schiller flashed me a look that said, *That's interesting*... Then he asked, "Why'd you do it, Holland? You spent eighteen years taking care of your brother, and then one day you just snapped."

Holland sighed long and deep, and the strength and life just seemed to slip out of him like a punctured airbed.

I knew from previous conversations that Holland had grown up believing in Mega-City One, in the Justice Department. He'd lost friends and family in the war—on both sides—but had never lost his faith in humanity. In the end, no matter what the odds, the good in people will triumph.

That's what he believed. That was at the core of Cadmus Robert Holland's being: the notion that people are inherently good. There are some who stray from time to time, but there is always a nucleus of goodness deep inside even the most hardened, most bloodthirsty criminal.

I guess he was right about that. Back in the Meg I got to know a lot of people who have one foot firmly in the gutter. The department classifies them as criminals, but ignores the good that they do. A woman can spend her entire life and all her money making clothes for the homeless, but she shoplifts one can of lettuce-freshener and she's labelled a thief.

I've already mentioned my friend Evan Quasarano. Grew up in the ghetto, joined a gang, became a small-time crook. Why'd he do that? Because he knew nothing else. His mother struggled to keep the family fed and clothed, his father was long gone and his grandfathers constantly bickered. They'd been on different sides during the war and every family get-together was destined to go down the 'What the *drokk* did you just say?' route. More than once I'd had to pry the two old guys apart, stop them from killing each other over the dinner table.

Evan was a thief, a thug, a lowlife numbers-runner and occasional bodyguard. All before his eighteenth birthday. Did that make him a bad person? No, just misguided. I'd spent a lot of time with him, listening to his barely-formed opinions and regurgitations of other people's ideas, and I could tell that Evan was just ignorant, and maybe a bit dumb. But I once saw him give half a bag of crawbies to a kid who'd had his own stash stolen before he could sell it, all because he knew that kid's mother would have beaten him if he'd come home empty-handed. You can't tell me *that's* something a bad person would do.

People are a little selfish, maybe, but when they take the time to step outside their own lives and see things from other perspectives, they generally do realise that we're all in this together. I'm not saying that it's altruism, doing good for no reward or recognition, but that's not the point. Every good thing we do helps make the world a better place—and who doesn't want to live in a better world?

That had always been Cadmus Holland's stance. Broderick—his younger brother—had apparently been a nice guy, doing pretty well at school, had some good friends. He'd been well-adjusted and well-liked by most people.

Holland said, "Something happened to him the day after a bunch of us went to the Festival of Wheels."

Schiller said, "I remember that. We couldn't go—Papa said it was too expensive to get to Mega-City One."

Holland nodded slowly for a moment, then calmly said, "You've been begging me forever to tell you, so shut the drokk up and listen."

Schiller grinned. He was never the sort to take offence easily.

"Broderick was thirteen years old," Holland said. "We'd had a good time at the festival but the next morning he didn't respond when I woke him up for school. I mean, he got up, but he didn't say anything. Went off to school still not talking to me. I figured he was angry with me for something, but you know kids—you can't read their minds. That night I got a call from his school. Broderick hadn't spoken to anyone all day, not even when his teachers asked him directly.

"So I went into his room and said, 'The hell's the matter with you?' Nothing. 'You're not talking to me?' Still nothing. I figured it would blow over in a few days, but I was wrong. I could see it in his eyes sometimes that he *wanted* to speak, but he just couldn't. I gave him a pencil and a pad, but he just threw them aside. Same with the datapad. After the second week I brought him to the doctor. Those first brain-scans alone cost me a month's salary, but they didn't show up anything wrong. No damage, no lesions, no parasites. Broderick had just lost the ability, or the will, to speak.

"We did have some medical insurance, but the drokkers refused to pay up without an official diagnosis, so I had to pay for everything. Sold the car. Sold the house to cover a four-week stint in the Tremaine Clinic, but still they couldn't find anything wrong. Had to move into a crappy one-bedroom stomm-hole on the west side after that. And then..." Holland looked up. "*That* day. Broderick was thirty. We'd been living with his condition for seventeen *years*. We were out, scouring the market down under the flyovers... I thought that maybe I could get him a job somewhere that it didn't matter that he couldn't speak. At that stage we were so broke I was dealing zizz to juves. So we saw this market stand where an old guy was selling dead-shirts. He—"

Kurya interrupted. "Dead-shirts?"

"Clothing taken from bodies at Resyk. Used to be that the Resyk centres just incinerated the stiffs' shoes and clothing, but then they started using it as landfill. Some people steal the clothes from the landfills and sell them. It was actually quite the fashion for a while. I remember—" I caught the look in Holland's eye. "Sorry. Go on."

Holland said, "I asked the old guy if he needed help getting the stuff, and he said, 'Yeah, maybe. Not easy work, though. You strong?' I said, 'I am, but it's not me looking for the job. It's my brother Broderick here.'

"And then Broderick said, 'It's about drokkin' time!'"

Kurya said, "So he had *not* lost the ability to speak?"

"No. No, he hadn't. I asked him what the hell was going on, and he told me that seventeen years earlier, the night before that first morning, just before he went to bed... We'd been joking about someone we knew. He didn't even remember *who* it was, but that's not important. What *is* important is that we both said, 'Yeah, that guy's *insane!*' at the same time. And... and then *I* said, 'Jinx.'"

We all stared at Holland.

Schiller muttered, "Stomm..."

I said, "No way. No *way* he kept that up for seventeen years!"

Holland said, "He did. Stubborn little *drokker*. That was the rule, see. Two of you say the same thing at the same time, then if one of you says 'jinx' before either of you say anything else, then the other one can't speak until the first one says their name."

Schiller asked, "In all that time you never said his name? Not even when you were speaking to a doctor about him?"

"Sure I did, but apparently not when he was around to hear me use it. He said I'd just referred to him as 'my brother.'" Holland stared down at his hands. "I'd put my entire life aside and spent every credit we had trying to find out what was wrong with him and he could have put a stop to it at any time with a note on a scrap of paper. So I hit him. And I couldn't stop. He was long dead by the time the Judges came, and even then they had to shoot me to get me away from him."

No one could think of anything to say after that.

Two

KELLAN WIGHTMAN CAUGHT up with me after the shift, as I was making my way back towards my cell.

"What was *that* about?" he asked, gesturing back towards the way he'd come. "Takenaga got a message on her datapad and muttered, 'Aw crap.' And then she just walked away."

"Since I wasn't there, I obviously have no idea," I said.

If Kalai Takenaga had been supervising him, that probably meant that Wightman had been on machine maintenance again. He usually griped about that, but I knew he secretly enjoyed it. Tinkering with an engine was a great way to lose yourself for a few hours.

Wightman was like me, a mod. A bulky man, taller than me and impressively strong. He sported a thick beard—now flecked with grey—in a futile attempt to hide the cybernetic modifications to his face. Wightman was coming to the end of his fifteenth year, almost half his sentence behind him, which was something he managed to bring up at every opportunity. "Two weeks from Wednesday and I'm over the crest of the hill," he said. "Fifteen whole *years* in this crap-cluster, can you believe that, Rico?"

"I've got seventeen to go, so, yeah." But I couldn't resent Wightman's buoyancy. Fifteen years without a shiv in the back was something of an achievement.

"We are gonna get absolutely stomm-faced," he said. "The stuff's been fermenting nicely. It should be pretty powerful. Probably tastes like what it is—rotten vegetables—but I don't care."

"Not for me," I said. "But knock yourself out. Which you probably will."

Wightman lowered his voice a little as we passed two anxious-looking guards. "We're not Judges any more, Rico. You can let go of the good-little-angel act."

Wightman had been on the job in Mega-City Two for eight years before he was arrested for setting fires in city blocks and then fabricating evidence to frame the Californian Secessionists. "Just a moment of madness," he'd said, the first time he talked to me about it. "Damn Fornies were causing so much trouble, something had to be done. It's not like I *murdered* anyone."

His 'moment of madness' had led him to torch seven city blocks, with damage estimated at the best part of half a billion credits. It was a wonder they hadn't executed him, and an absolute miracle more people hadn't died.

The only reason he got caught was because he'd always taken great care to ensure that each block's alarm systems were fully functioning to make sure that everyone go out before the fire really took hold. But on that seventh block the alarms worked fine for the first minute, then abruptly shut off. By that stage it was too late to quench the fire. Wightman risked his own life getting everyone out. Four of them later died due to severe smoke inhalation.

I'm not saying that getting all those people out makes him a hero—I mean, he'd started the damn fires himself—but he wasn't technically a murderer.

Wightman had settled into prison life neatly. He quickly became the prison's chief booze-hound. He knew alcohol inside and out, and there was a running joke that the guy could ferment a sack. He had the advantage that most of the other prisoners were Judges with little experience of real alcohol, so even a thimbleful of the hard stuff was enough to get them swaying.

"You'll like the latest batch," he said. "Grapefruit wine. It's been ready for weeks, but this is a celebration, so I want it to be something special. Fermentation can only get you so far. Now I'm looking into distillation."

"There is no way you can build a still and not have the guards find it," I said.

"Don't need to. Distillation is just separating the alcohol from the water, right? Don't need to evaporate the stuff to do that. The freezing point of alcohol is negative one hundred fourteen degrees. So I'll drop the temperature to about negative eight"—Wightman's sewn-up lips formed into a rudimentary smile—"the water freezes, but the alcohol doesn't. Then I'll just take out the ice."

That sounded right, but I still didn't want to get involved.

It wasn't that I was afraid of reprisals: I just wasn't interested in getting drunk. It was important that I kept my head clear. Most of the time the prison was peaceful, but that was only because ninety per cent of the prisoners were biding their time before they made whatever moves they felt were vital to their own well-being.

Fights could, and did, break out seemingly spontaneously, but luckily few of them descended into full-scale riots: that was when this place got *really* dangerous.

The unspoken prison hierarchy would be upset for a day or two, then settle down again. The big storm disaster that led to me becoming a mod had wiped out the prison's most sadistic guards and some of the worst of the prisoners, but the power vacuum was filled in a matter of weeks.

I could have seized power then, probably, but I chose not to, because while *technically* I was a criminal, I wasn't a crook. I was one of the good guys.

So my reputation kept the small-fry clear of me, but it attracted the bruisers. You don't want to be drunk when someone is charging at you with a shiv.

And there was one bruiser in particular who'd been gunning for me. Southern Brennan. He'd come in on the last ship, and the first thing he did was put out the word that he wanted my head on a pike.

Brennan was one of the biggest guys I'd ever seen that wasn't a mutant. His fist was the size of my head. He hadn't even made it all the way through the Academy of Law before he'd committed so many brutal crimes that he was shipped straight to Titan. I heard that he once threw a Lawmaster at another cadet. I dunno about that; a Lawmaster weighs the best part of a tonne.

Someone screwed up in the cadet screening process, that was certain. Or maybe something happened to him along the way, something that changed him. I guess that's more likely, because cadets go through stringent psych tests right from the start. Brennan's aberrations would have been caught a lot sooner if they'd been there all along.

Anyway. The reason I bring him up now is that as Wightman and I were walking, Brennan appeared at the far end of the corridor.

Wightman muttered a few select swear words and there was a definite hesitation in his step, but I kept going. I knew what I was doing. Keep a steady pace. Don't try to stare Brennan down, but don't ignore him either.

I'd done this before, a couple of years earlier, shortly after I became a mod. A similar situation: a guy who wanted my intestines between his teeth solely because everyone knew that mods were hard to kill. In that case, I was able to put him off for months by telling him, "Not now. This is not the time, and you know that." Kept that up for ages, until one day he was expecting me to do the same as I passed him on the way down into one of the northern mineshafts. Idiot. You never tell a man you want to kill him and then let your guard down. They found his body after a brief search at the end of the shift. All the signs indicated that he'd snagged his environment suit on something and for unknown reasons he'd ignored the suit's low-pressure warnings.

Now Southern Brennan was striding towards me, and I could tell that Wightman was ready to turn and run. But he held his ground. I was proud of him for that.

Brennan was flanked by Vivean Kassir and Lorne Sims, both former Mega-City One Judges. They'd adopted him into their little clique, nurtured his psychopathic tendencies to use him as a weapon. It hadn't worked the way they'd planned: they'd made the mistake of assuming that Brennan's size and strength were balanced by a lack of brains.

Now Brennan stopped in front of me, and Sims and Kassir spread out a little, making it very clear that Wightman and I were not expected to simply step around them.

We were about four metres away when Brennan called out, "You *cosy* in there, Rico Dredd?"

I slowed to a stop, regarded him as casually as I would if anyone else had asked me the time. "Meaning?"

"You keep to yourself, feeling all safe and snug and protected. Tucked away in the warden's pocket. You think we don't know? Comes to a fight, Rico doesn't take sides because he's already on the side of the establishment."

I was watching Brennan as he spoke, and it was hard to focus on his words because the man was just so damn huge. He was a head taller than me, and I'm no shrimp. Zero body fat. He looked like he'd been sculpted by someone who'd accidentally bought enough muscle for four people and didn't want to waste anything.

"You're wrong about that," I said. "I *do* take a side. Mine."

"They say you went out into the Bronze with twenty-five others and you're the only one who made it back." He took a step closer, and peered down at me. "You kill them?"

"What do you want, Brennan?"

"Same thing *every* drokker in this place wants."

"Freedom."

He shook his head. "Freedom's just a point of view. What we want is control over our own lives. I aim to regain mine. A lot of people are going to get in my way. I think you're going to be one of them, so I'm putting you on notice right now." He tilted his head closer to mine, and I could almost hear the muscles in his neck creaking against each other. "You're either on my side or in my way. There's no neutral ground. You make your choice, Dredd." He stepped back and glanced around. "And make it fast. All of this will come crashing down."

On Brennan's left, Lorne Sims said, "I wouldn't trust this drokker if he told me stomm was sticky."

Brennan calmly looked at me for a few more seconds, then said, "You think you're a tough guy, Rico. I can see that in you. You think you're top dog here, that nothing can touch you, because you and Copus made some kind of deal after you got back from the Bronze. You're going to tell me what that is."

A voice from the far end of the corridor yelled out, "The hell is this, blockin' the corridors? Keep *movin*', you drokkers!"

Brennan quietly said, "De Luyando. He'll be the first to go."

I tried not to sneer as I said, "Right. When you seize control of a prison mining colony that'll fall apart without support from a homeworld a billion kilometres away."

De Luyando yelled, "I said *move*, you spugwits! You want me to come over there and *make* you move?"

Brennan turned around, muttering, "Pick a side, Dredd. I won't tell you again." He strode away, Sims and Kassir almost running to keep up.

Wightman—when he was sure that Brennan was out of earshot—asked me, "How the hell did that animal get so close to making Judge?"

There was no answering that. The same question had been asked about me, and probably a good number of the other prisoners on Titan. How could an institution as strictly controlled and as heavily monitored as the Mega-City One Academy of Law produce Judges who are anything less than perfect? For fifteen years, every aspect of our lives is scheduled, studied and logged. There's almost nothing a cadet can do that falls outside the attention of the system.

When my class was seven years old—Joe and I were the *equivalent* of seven, roughly, but it's hard to be accurate because of the accelerated ageing process—Cadet Sabrina Han quietly told me that she hated Judge-Tutor Rowley. There was no one else around, and I never mentioned it to anyone, but the next morning Rowley strode up to Han and told her, "We're not here to be liked, Han. We're here to teach you. You don't like that, you can quit. Is *that* what you are, Han? A quitter?"

I don't know, maybe Han had told someone else, and they'd mentioned it to Rowley. Still, the incident stands out in my memory as the first time I realised that my life wasn't my own. The Justice Department owned everything about me, even down to the thoughts in my head. For a long time I was afraid to even think of anything negative about the tutors or the training, just in case. And this was *before* I understood about psychics.

Wightman kept his voice low as we passed the scowling De Luyando. "Rico, if you *had* to take down Brennan, how would you do it? I'm not saying it will come to that, but if it does."

"Balls, throat, and eyes, in that order," I said. "Simplest, quickest way to take him off the board."

"Jovus, that's cold. You go for a guy's eyes and miss, he is *not* going to let that slide. There's no going back from that."

"You think I'm the sort of person who'd beat someone into submission so that later we can be pals?"

"No, but... I mean, you might need them later, right? Say you were going to try to take control of the prison. You can't kill *everyone* who stood against you, because that'd be all the wardens and guards, and they're the ones who know how to keep the lights on and the air working."

"Kellan, we're not talking about this," I told him. "Seriously. We are prisoners here for good reason. There's not one of us who doesn't deserve this."

He stopped walking and stared at me. I had to stop too: didn't want anyone else listening in on whatever he was about to say next. I knew what it was going to be, though.

"Even you?"

"I broke the law."

"But you said that the laws you broke were unfair. The *system* is unfair."

"Come on..." I nodded in the direction we'd been walking, and Wightman fell into step beside me. "Look, I still broke the law. Doesn't matter how wrong a law is. If you break it willingly, you have to be prepared to pay the price." I could see that he still wasn't getting it. "Wightman, from the minute I hit the streets I tried to subvert the Department of Justice's training. I thought I knew better, that their way was too restrictive, too inhuman."

"And now you don't? Three years here have changed your mind?"

"No. I was right then, and I'm still right. But if you take an action—regardless of the nature of that action, or the reason you've chosen to take it—and you're fully aware of its impact and possible consequences, then you can't complain if you end up *suffering* those consequences."

The corridor opened onto the transparent plasteen tunnel linking the prison's administrative quarters to the hydroponic domes. On a clear day you could see the sun sinking behind Saturn, its light rippling through the rings. A breathtaking sight. But this was not a clear day. Visibility was down to about five hundred metres, I guessed. Titan's atmosphere was brown, cold, dark. It was hard to shake the impression that there was oil in the water and grit in the clouds.

Wightman said, "I'm beginning to think maybe you *like* it here, Rico."

I snorted, as well as anyone with mechanical lungs can snort.

"Seriously. You weren't even on the streets for a *year* before they arrested you. I think that maybe you became institutionalised in the Academy of Law. There's no way to return to that once you graduate, so you put yourself in a position to get arrested and imprisoned. There's not much difference between the Academy and this place, if you look at it in a certain way."

I honestly hadn't considered that before. He was wrong, I was sure, but only an idiot dismisses an idea just because it makes them uncomfortable.

I told him, "If you look at *any* two things in the right light, you can find similarities. That's cherry-picking, Kellan. Shouting excitedly about the few similarities while brushing the many differences under the carpet is like trying to convince a fish that it can live in gasoline. Gasoline and water are both liquids, both have hydrogen as a key element, you can store them both in buckets."

"That doesn't mean I'm wrong."

"That's true," I said. "But I *don't* like it here, any more than you do." I held out my hands, palms-up. "Look what they've done to us."

Wightman glanced at his own hands, but didn't say anything. He'd never spoken of the reason behind his own transformation, but others had told me.

He'd been out on the surface, part of a chain gang slowly sweeping across what had once possibly been a lake-bed. A scan had detected iridium deposits on the surface and the initial on-the-ground survey had provided confirmation: at some point in the past thousand years a very large iridium-heavy asteroid had skimmed the atmosphere; chunks of it had broken off and deposited an estimated nine billion credits' worth of the precious metal across the surface. The easiest and cheapest way to find and retrieve the fragments was the chain gang: fifty prisoners chained together for four days, carefully sieving through the sand- and dust-covered lake-bed.

On the third day, Wightman had noticed that his environment suit was telling him its urine pack was full. He signalled to the nearest guard and said, "Need to purge here, chief."

"Not now," he was told. "Shift ends in four hours twenty. Hold it."

"I *have* been holding it, chief," Wightman had replied. "All morning. It'll auto-purge if I don't—"

"Just keep working, Wightman."

After another hour of ignoring his suit's signals that the artificial bladder was dangerously full, Wightman again asked for permission, and was again denied.

Ten minutes later, he decided drokk it, what were they going to do? Fire him? He turned around and released the bladder's valve. The stream of urine had been under more pressure than he'd realised, and in Titan's low gravity it arced out pretty far. The urine froze almost instantly, of course, but it still had momentum and mass.

It hit another guard square in the back of his helmet. I haven't read the report but it's easy to guess that the guard thought he was under attack.

He spun around and opened fire. His shot drilled a hole in Wightman's chest and emerged between his shoulder blades, then passed straight through his oxygen tank.

It was practically a miracle that Wightman didn't die before they got him back to the prison. As it was, he suffered oxygen deprivation, hypothermia and severe blood loss. Turning him into a mod was the only way to save his life. No, let me be more accurate: it was the only way to save his life that would leave him still able to work.

I knew he didn't accept what they'd done to him, that the sense of betrayal and horror and loss had never left him.

As we walked through the transparent tunnel—only occasionally glancing up to see if there was a break in the clouds—he said, "I'm going to sue them, soon as I set foot on Earth. I heard that when the Titan shuttle comes in to San Fran, there are solicitors just waiting for the prisoners. They're all desperate to make media-deals and help the parolees sue anyone and everyone they can. And what with the hard-luck aspect you can double your income if you're a mod, is what I heard. 'They turned me into a monster' kind of thing."

"*Has* anyone ever successfully sued the Department of Justice?" I asked.

"Probably not. And I probably won't be successful either. But I'm going to do it anyway. Make a big noise about how they've treated me."

"Maybe it would work in Mega-City Two, but not where I come from. We got rid of most of the lawyers back when—"

Wightman slapped my upper arm and pointed ahead. "What's this?"

Three guards were striding quickly towards us from the hydroponic domes. "You tell me," I said. Wightman had much better eyesight than I did—the modification process isn't exactly precision engineering.

"Giambalvo, McConnach and Sloane. And they're looking at us."

We both stopped walking. That was just something every prisoner learned to do, one of those unwritten, unspoken rules. If a guard doesn't give you a direct order to approach, you stand still and let them come to you. I never thought about it much, but I guess that subconsciously you're expecting a fight, so letting the guard cover the distance, however short it might be, is a way of ensuring that they've expended more energy than you have before the potential trouble begins.

When they were close enough that they didn't have to shout, sub-warden Giambalvo said, "You two. Warden's office. Right now."

Wightman said, "What for? We haven't done—"

McConnach's daystick lanced out, striking Wightman square on the voicebox. He staggered back, then dropped to his knees, gagging and groaning. I've had that done to me more than once—by McConnach herself—and it hurts like you've been gargling chunks of broken glass.

"After fifteen years anyone would think that you'd learn, Wightman," McConnach said. "Your days of giving orders are long over."

Giambalvo looked at me. "We don't have time for drokking around," she said. "Pick up your friend and come with us."

Three

In the three years since I'd arrived on Titan I'd only twice seen the warden in person. Governor Myles Dodge, seventy, completely bald—didn't even have eyebrows—with African and Caucasian heritage. He had the look of an old-time circus strongman whose body had finally succumbed to age: a broad frame supporting a body draped with far too much loose skin.

It was easy to get the impression that Dodge spent his days sitting in his office watching TV while he left the running of the prison to the sub-wardens and guards, and maybe that was the impression he *wanted* to give, for some reason. But the fact is he had his finger on the pulse, as I'd learned the first time I met him.

That had been shortly after my modification surgery. I was in the infirmary, with sub-warden Copus in the middle of explaining certain truths to me, when the door opened and Dodge entered.

He looked me up and down, and said to Copus, "Good job. What does he remember?"

"About the process? Nothing."

I said, "Who the hell are you?"

He ignored that, and asked Copus, "Who was on the airlock when he was brought in?"

"Giambalvo." Copus hesitated for a second. "So far she's said nothing, but I don't know her well enough to trust her."

"I do. She can keep her mouth shut." He turned to me. "Dredd, I'm Governor Dodge. You understand why we did this to you?"

"Sure, I understand." He looked as though he didn't believe me, so I repeated it more firmly. "I understand. The other inmates have to believe that Titan is so hostile that this was the only way to save my life." I shrugged. "I hate it, but I get it. If they believe there's even the slightest chance of surviving out there, they'll spend all their time plotting their escape. That's not going to get the ore out of the ground, and the ore is the only thing that makes this place viable."

Dodge watched me as I spoke, nodding slowly, then said, "Your voicebox gives you an advantage over non-modified prisoners, Dredd; it's harder to tell whether you think I'm a piece of toast. So we're going to have to judge you by your actions, not your words. Work hard and keep your head down, and you might find yourself in my favour. The journey from Earth to Titan is expensive, so anything less than a twenty-year sentence is just not cost-effective... But say an inmate was to help keep the peace. Fewer fights means fewer injuries. That means fewer days in the infirmary and lower running costs. Something like that might weigh heavily in your favour, Dredd. It's all economics. Do you understand what I'm saying?"

"I do. Aside from the reference to toast."

Copus said, "Don't butter him up."

"Right, got it."

Dodge continued, "Then there's the opposite approach. Push against the system, the system pushes back, and no one man—no matter *how* impressed he is with himself—can win against the system."

He tapped the centre of his chest with his index finger. "The system. In case there's any confusion."

The second time I met Governor Dodge was sixteen months later, when former EuroCit Judge Ren Tramatky lifted a guard's gun and managed to deactivate its handprint scanner. Exactly how he did that we still don't know, but the result was chaos: two guards dead and fourteen wounded, six prisoners wounded, and more than fifty almost suffocated when Tramatky realised there was no possible way to escape and blasted a hole in the mess-hall windows. I'd ordered Wightman and a couple of others to block the cracked windows with tables and plastic trays while I took down Tramatky with my bare fists. Afterwards, Dodge had called me to his office to—he said—commend me on my quick thinking. I figured he was checking up on me. Wanted to look me in the eye, see if he could work out what I was thinking. And maybe because the whole hands-off image he worked so hard to maintain kept him a further step removed from what was happening on the ground. He asked me to explain what had happened, how I thought Tramatky might have disabled the handprint scanner—I didn't have an answer for that one—and if there was anything else I wanted to report. I wasn't able to think of anything that might fit, so after a few awkward exchanges he concluded that we were done, and he dismissed me.

It wasn't until months later that I realised the real reason Myles Dodge had called me in. He liked me. Liked my company. Unlike most of the prisoners, I wasn't permanently arrogant or terrified. I wasn't raging against the system that put me there. I'd accepted that they'd made me into a mod without too much in the way of complaint.

And maybe there was a philosophical connection too: pretty early in his career, Dodge had been wounded during a riot at an aeroball stadium: spine broken in four places. He'd never quite recovered, and had spent the next decade driving a desk, despite his protestations that he was strong enough to return to the streets.

Then in 2076, Governor Nkambule decided to see what bullets tasted like, and her job was suddenly vacant... and tantalising for Dodge. Solid work, a twenty-year contract with the option to retire at the end of it, and a hefty pension.

Judges don't normally get paid, but the mining corporations on the outer planets' moons are multinational, so they don't answer to any one city. Plus it's hard to persuade *anyone* to go, so the corporations tell potential guards and wardens, "We'll put your salary aside for you, every month, in a high-interest account. When your term is done and you come back to Earth, you'll get it all in one lump sum. You'll never have to work another day in your life."

And for Dodge there was the added attraction of Titan's low gravity, about a seventh of that on Earth. Sure, inside the prison we had grav-plates on the floor to make it easier to get around, but they were rarely running at full-G. That had to be bliss for someone who's suffered decades of back pain.

So I got to thinking that maybe Dodge saw something of himself in me: we'd both wanted to be Judges, but the system wasn't flexible enough to accept that we differed from the standard model of a Judge.

I don't know, maybe I'm wrong about that. Certainly, Dodge didn't seem to have anything like that on his mind when Giambalvo and the others escorted me and Wightman into his office.

Sub-warden Copus was already there, standing beside Dodge's desk with his arms folded and his brow furrowed. And so was Zera Kurya.

Copus said, "This is everyone," but I couldn't tell from his tone whether that was a statement or a question.

Governor Dodge looked around, nodded, and said, "We have a situation, and you people are going to resolve it. Four days ago a freighter outbound towards Mimas suffered a catastrophic failure. Its crew managed to regain enough control to steer it towards Titan. One hour ago it breached our atmosphere. That slowed its descent a little, but not enough. It hit the ground *hard*... and our long-range scanners are picking up possible life signs." He looked directly at me. "You and Wightman are going out to find the crash site and retrieve any survivors and supplies. Kurya is here because back in East-Meg One she was a top-rated Med-Judge."

Wightman said, "Yeah... I don't *think* so. I've just come off a shift. There's no law that says we have to..." He noticed Dodge's scowl and slowed to a stop. "Damn it. All right."

I asked, "Where did the ship hit?"

"A few kilometres south of Brunel's Ridge."

I knew enough about Titan's geography to get an inkling of what we were facing. "That's got to be five hundred kilometres from here."

Giambalvo said, "Closer to *six* hundred."

Copus glanced at Dodge—who very slightly shook his head—then he turned back to us. "Since our friends in Texas-City have yet to deliver on the shuttles they promised us eight drokkin' *years* ago, we've got to go overland. The rescue party is the seven of us here. Not counting the warden, of course."

Giambalvo said, "Sir, I can't. The low gravity outside... you know how much it affects me. I was invalided out of the Department because my sense of balance is shot to stomm. In the low gravity it gets even worse."

"The transport has grav-plates, Giambalvo. You'll be okay."

"I won't be able to function effectively. I recommend Takenaga take my place. She understands discretion. Plus she's logged more time on the surface than I have."

Copus exchanged another look with Dodge, but this time the warden nodded. "All right," Copus said. "Find her, brief her. Sloane, you're the driver—get down to the compound and requisition the best vehicle you can find. Nothing smaller than a four-tonne. The freighter's complement is seventeen. It's unlikely that they all survived, but we have to prepare for that."

Sloane said, "The *big* bus would do it..." He checked his watch. "It's due to head out on the next shift."

"Okay. Tell the quartermaster to talk to me if he gives you any trouble."

As Sloane and Giambalvo left, Copus turned to me, Wightman and Kurya. "You all know how dangerous it is out there. We're aware that with danger there comes opportunity. Any of you even *think* about turning on us, you'll find yourselves—"

Kurya cut him off. "We understand. We are still prisoners."

Wightman asked, "Just wondering, chief. Do we get anything for this? I mean, we're risking our lives."

Governor Dodge said, "We'll talk about that when you return. They..."

He looked away as his voice trailed off, and that was when I knew that they were lying. This was not a rescue mission.

This was something else.

Something a lot more dangerous.

Four

"The Big Bus" was the name given to the prison's most powerful vehicle. It wasn't the largest—that was our General Dynamics H88 Crawler, which could haul a hundred tonnes of ore at a maximum speed of fifteen kilometres per hour—and it wasn't the fastest, which was a Mega-City One Justice Department Lawmaster that had been modified to run on sand. We only had one of those, and it wasn't going to be much use for this mission.

The Big Bus was a double-width version of our standard personnel carrier. Range of over three thousand kilometres and capable of carrying a hundred passengers in relative comfort, if all the seats were installed, one-sixty in misery if they weren't.

The reason it was double-width—actually wider than it was long—was that it had once been two standard vehicles, and some engineering genius had bolted them together. The original plan had been to join them end-to-end, but the surface of Titan is pitted with so many crevasses and craters that the long bus would have got stuck every time it crested a hill.

Wightman knew a lot more about engineering than I did, and he'd always wanted to travel on the Big Bus.

In the airlock, as we waited for Kurya to seal her environment suit, Wightman was growing more and more excited, like a kid on his Birthday Eve. "You know how intricate a differential gearbox is in a normal vehicle? This one has got to be ten times as complex!"

He took the lead as we left the prison's hangar and headed towards the bus. Not caring whether or not Kurya and I understood—or cared—he launched into his lecture: "Your standard wheeled car has wheels on both sides, right? This means that when it's turning, the wheels on the inside of the curve have a shorter distance to travel than those on the *outside* of the curve, which means they have to turn slower. Now, in most cases only the rear wheels have drive—the front ones aren't connected to the engine. So when it's turning, the front wheels can turn however much they need to, no problems there, but the rear wheels are connected to the engine via a common drive-shaft. So the whole mechanism needs to work in a way that the engine provides different rates of power to the inside and outside wheels. It gets even more complicated with a four-wheel-drive vehicle." We'd reached the bus; Wightman had already dropped to his knees and was peering underneath the chassis. "But in this case it's *way* more complicated because all the wheels are driven—"

"We get it," I told him.

Wightman twisted around and lowered himself onto his back, started shimmying underneath the bus. "Man, I'd love to see the schematics for this. Two separate engines, sixteen wheels, four drive-shafts! Just the braking system is giving me palpitations! I tell you I was planning to retrain as a Tek-Judge? I always got along better with machines than with people." He drew up his legs, dug his heels into the dirt, then pushed himself further under the bus. "Rico, go get me a flashlight. I want to see how they've linked up the two suspension systems."

Kurya nudged my arm, and I looked up to see Copus and Takenaga approaching, cautiously making their way across the packed-dirt ground.

I kicked the sole of Wightman's boot. "No time for that. Come on."

Copus seemed particularly unsteady, but I quickly realised why. As second-in-command to Dodge he delegated work to the other wardens. He rarely left the prison himself, and wasn't used to the low gravity.

"Move it," Copus barked at us. "Departing in ninety seconds."

I grabbed Wightman's ankle and dragged him back out.

We followed Kurya onto the bus, and the engines coughed into life as the airlock doors closed and sealed behind us.

Guard Ernie Sloane was at the controls, flipping switches and checking read-outs more efficiently than usual. Copus was standing with his back to the windshield, already removing his helmet. McConnach was near the back, kneeling on one seat while she rummaged through an emergency pack on the seat behind it, and in the alcove behind Sloane, Takenaga was checking the seals on the weapons rack.

Copus said, "Sit down, strap in, and hold on tight. We've got a lot of ground to cover and not a lot of time."

Takenaga asked, "So what *is* this? Giambalvo said something about a crashed freighter."

"Not yet." Copus glanced at Sloane. "Gun it."

I'd barely lowered myself into a seat before the bus surged forward.

In the seat in front of me, Wightman muttered, "Holy crap!" and turned around to stare at me with wide eyes. "Talk about *torque!* I had no idea this bugger could move this fast!"

Sloane called back, "We should hit a cruising speed of about one-thirty, but the topographical data beyond the four-hundred-K radius is pretty sketchy. Rough estimate for our ETA—and don't hold me to this—is approximately six hours."

Takenaga said, "ETA already has the word 'estimated' in there. You don't need to repeat it, much less add 'rough' and 'approximately.'"

Sloane laughed. "Hah, yeah. That does sound a bit vague, doesn't it? But we're going to be crossing *terra incognita* so there's no way of knowing what we're going to hit."

Softly, Takenaga said, "Can't be *terra* incognita. This isn't *Terra.*"

Wightman winked at me and whispered, "Remember I told you she was pedantic?"

Copus called out, "All right, everyone listen up. McConnach? I'm talking to you too."

"Double-checking the supplies, boss," she called back. "We're supposed to do it *before* we leave, but—"

"Turn around and pay attention, McConnach. Now."

My guts started to churn. They'd already been troubling me, but now they were hitting the spin-cycle.

Copus said, "Mister Sloane, disengage the vehicle's radio, GPS tracking, and the transponder."

"Eh... No."

"Do it, Mister Sloane. That's an order."

"Sir, if I do that, then I'm driving blind. It's not like there are road signs on this planet."

Takenaga muttered "moon" under her breath.

Copus said, "I didn't say disable the GPS *entirely*, just the tracking. I don't want anyone to know exactly where we've been or be able to retrace our path. That's why we're maintaining radio silence until we're back at the mine."

Sloane hesitated, but flipped some switches next to the steering column. "Okay. It's done."

"Good." Copus looked around at the rest of us. "There is no freighter."

We watched in silence as he passed a handwritten note to Sloane. "Stay on your current vector until you reach these coordinates, then head due south. Top speed."

Sloane began, "But this isn't—"

"Shut up. Just drive. And listen." Copus looked at each of us in turn. "The freighter is a cover story in case any of you decided not to participate. The real story is that twelve hundred kilometres south of the prison there is a small but vital military complex." Using the backs of the seats to steady himself, he moved forward until he was standing only a metre away from Takenaga, staring at her. "It's jointly run by the three North American Mega-Cities, and its existence is in violation of fourteen separate international charters and directives on extra-terrestrial military establishments."

From the back of the bus McConnach asked, "*Aliens?*"

"No, I mean extra-terrestrial as in 'not situated on Earth.' After the war every nation agreed to certain limitations on firepower and presence outside the planet." Copus returned his attention to Takenaga. "Hondo City does not know of the existence of this base. Do you understand, Kalai?"

She nodded. "Of course."

Copus hesitated for a second, then said, "We need to be clear about this. I'm not asking if you understand that the base exists and that it is secret. I'm asking whether you understand that it must *remain* a secret."

Again, she nodded.

"I want a verbal response, Kalai. And an affirmation that you will not inform your superiors of its existence."

"I understand, sub-warden, and I promise that I will say nothing."

Next, Copus turned to Kurya. "And you?"

A lot of the time it was hard to tell with Kurya whether she was even listening, let alone paying attention, but she nodded and said, "I have twenty-seven years remaining on my sentence. I have no doubt that by the time I return home and face my former superiors, your military base will either have already served its purpose or been exposed by some other means."

Wightman and I exchanged a glance. That was by far the most we'd ever heard Kurya say in one go.

Copus was about to respond when Kurya continued: "That said, I could easily inform other prisoners of the base's existence, and it's conceivable that one of those prisoners would return to Earth and inform my superiors. If you truly wish your base to remain secret, you should instead work to establish a bond of mutual trust, dependency or fear between all seven of us currently in this vehicle."

Copus nodded and said, "Right..."

I figured it was time to speak up. "Kurya's right, boss. I've known about the base for a couple of years and said nothing to anyone, because you made it worth my while to keep my mouth shut." I tapped at my sealed lips to reinforce the irony.

Wightman glared at me. "How the hell did *you* find out about it? Wait, was this back when you were trapped out there and...?" He frowned. "I always kinda wondered how you made it back to the prison on your own. You said it was just sheer determination, but that doesn't fill oxygen tanks, does it? So what happened, they rescued you?"

"I didn't know for *sure* that there was a base, but I figured there had to be something. Our hydroponics produce more food than we need, so what happens to the excess?"

Kurya said, “How you deduced the existence of the base is irrelevant. I am naturally curious about its purpose...” She looked at Copus. “But more curious about this *mission*.”

Five

Copus told us that he didn't know much. He'd never visited the base, never had direct contact with any of its personnel, didn't know a lot about it other than that it existed.

About once every six days one of the prison trucks was loaded up with food and supplies from the hydroponic farms and dropped off at a pre-arranged location. I'd already worked that out, a long time ago, but never had the means or the chance to find out much more than that.

Copus said, "There's a shielded comm-link between the base and the prison. A *physical* line, not just a radio link. It has one purpose: to send a distress signal. The only people who know about it are Governor Dodge, Giambalvo and myself. The long-standing agreement is that in the event of an emergency—an uncontrollable riot, an invasion, a natural disaster that threatens the safety of the prison—we trigger the alarm and they come to our aid." He glanced at me. "Got to say, the closest we came to hitting it was when your party went missing."

Sloane snorted. "I'm guessing that you never expected the alarm to go both ways."

"Correct," Copus said. "Twenty-eight minutes ago we received a video signal through that channel from Captain Apolla Harrow." He triggered a holo-projection, and a frozen image of a wide-eyed, pale-skinned woman appeared in the air beside him. She was too close to the camera to see much behind her other than part of a wall and the edge of a doorway. "We're assuming that she was in command, but we've no way of knowing that for certain. Sound's missing for the first few seconds."

He played the message, and the holo rushed into life. Harrow spun around to check behind her, then turned back. She silently mouthed something, then briefly looked behind her again. She was clearly anticipating something bad.

McConnach said, "She's scared."

Before anyone else could respond, the sound kicked in. "—the drokk *out* before he kills us all! I repeat: This is Huygens Base. We have a *code red* situation and require *immediate* assistance! At least eight dead with—" Something flashed behind Harrow and an exit wound appeared in her chest. As she toppled forward, the projection froze again.

"That's all we've got," Copus said.

We sat in silence for a few moments, then Takenaga asked, "How do you know her name? We can't see her tunic label from this angle, and even if we could, it would only show her surname."

"Governor Dodge identified her," Copus said. He dropped into the nearest seat and turned to rest his arm on the seat's back as he faced us. "She sent him a comm through standard channels a few years back. He said it stuck in his memory because he had no idea who she was or why she'd established contact, and then his reply got bounced."

I said, "So she was sowing seeds just in case she ever needed him. Smart." I gestured towards the spot in the air where the projection had been. "Can you show us again, boss? Run it at quarter speed, see if there's anything else we can get from it."

Over the next hour, we watched the footage four more times, then frame-by-frame, all the while picking out anything that might be relevant.

It was McConnach who spotted that the faded and heavily scraped-away writing on the wall-panels behind Harrow was originally the phrase '*Until Inner Door Is Sealed.*' "She's in an airlock, no doubt about it."

Wightman said that the panels themselves were not what you'd expect to see in an established base: "That's a ship. Military, is my guess. The holo is too low-res to be sure, but I think we're looking at foamed-steel panels. There used to be a manufacturing station in the asteroid belt that specialised in foamed-steel. It's very light, very strong, and can only be made in a zero-g environment. But it costs three times as much as standard steel or titanium plating, so it's really only the military that can afford it. You wouldn't use it to build a base."

Takenaga said, "She used the word 'he' but didn't give a name. That implies that it's someone she knows."

My own contribution to the discussion seemed pretty minor at first. "The camera didn't move. That means it's fixed, not hovering or being held. And she was shot from behind... Could be they knew what she was doing and wanted to stop the message from getting out. Or they were not thinking clearly for whatever reason."

But it was Zera Kurya who spotted something that the rest of us were kicking ourselves for missing. "Captain Harrow broke radio silence so obviously this is a drastic situation; but she did not mention the prison. Her demeanour indicates that she was not in the right mindset for subterfuge, making it unlikely that she was hiding the recipient of her message. We cannot conclude with any certainty that the prison was the intended recipient."

I said, "Okay... But the comm link between Huygens and the prison is isolated, so no one is going to pick up that message by accident. If Harrow was hoping to contact her superiors on Earth—or someone else; who knows?—they didn't get the message." I looked up at Copus. "What's the base's complement?"

He shrugged. "Unknown."

Wightman said, "Well, it's at least eight people fewer than it was yesterday."

Sloane called out, "Hold tight—we're on those coords. Making a sharp left now."

I'd half expected a brief countdown, but Sloane wasn't playing around: we were all immediately flung to the right, and for a few seconds my stomach threatened to heave as the bus's grav-plating struggled to keep up with the shifting g-force.

When our path had straightened out, Copus said, "Jovus, Ernie! Next time, give us a heads-up!"

Sloane sighed theatrically. "Gotcha, boss..." He lowered his voice a little, but not so I couldn't hear him. "Reckon you shouldn't engage Dredd and the others. They're prisoners, for Grud's sake. Murderers. We can't trust a word they say." He glanced over his shoulder at me. "Especially *that* drokker. If he told me my name was Ernie Sloane, I'd contact my mother to check, and even then I wouldn't believe her."

"These three were Judges," Copus said, "just like us."

"Yeah? Well, forgive my candour, boss, but they turned their backs on their Justice Departments. Sold them out."

Takenaga laughed. "So did *we*, Sloane. There's not one of us here because we love guarding prisoners. We're here because we love getting paid."

"Enough," Copus said. "Rico, you were making a point?"

"Just that if very few people in the prison know about the comm link, could be true at the base too. The grunts know that the prison exists, but not about the link. They might be expecting aid from another military outfit. That could take days."

They all took a moment for that to sink in, then Takenaga said, "There are military and research bases on Jupiter, the asteroid belt and Mars—and probably a few in between—but Huygens Base is covert; even in an emergency they won't risk compromising it. Earth is about eighty light-minutes from Saturn, on average. That's two hours forty minimum to send a radio message and receive a response... Upshot is, even if there *was* a team geared up and ready to go on the next closest base, the message would still have to be relayed from Earth, and the team would have to *get* here. Unless there's a military ship in orbit right *now*, my guess is the earliest Huygens can expect backup is two days." She looked around and saw the rest of us staring at her. "What? I'm a military buff."

Copus nodded slowly at that. "So there's a chance they have no idea that we're coming."

"That's what I'm thinking," I said. "And we don't know what's there waiting for us. So unless some new intel shows up before we get there, I think we need to approach with extreme caution. If some hostile force has taken the base and they have access to military weaponry—judging by the distance from the airlock door and the size of the exit-wound in Harrow's chest, that gun was at least a point-five-oh calibre—then we're potentially walking into a firestorm."

McConnach pulled herself out of her seat and moved to the seat across from me. "Dredd's right. We don't know the situation, the topography, or *anything* about the base itself. For all we know there could be a thousand trigger-happy grunts there who're going to open fire on any unknown vehicle that gets too close—including us. They could be already tracking us."

That was a sobering thought.

I remained silent for a while, letting the problem stew in the back of my brain as I half listened to the others making plans for what they hoped was the most likely situation.

Between them Takenaga and Wightman worked out that Huygens Base couldn't hold more than eighty personnel, based on the amount of food that we supplied. That gave them a starting point. Assuming twenty-four square metres per person, that made the base around two thousand square metres in area.

"Sounds about right for an office," said Copus. "But military bases have crew quarters and vehicle hangars and weapons storage. So I reckon we can double it. Four thousand square metres."

"That's floor space," McConnach said. "It won't be a conveniently rectangular single-storey building, will it? It'll be multiple floors. Some of the base could be underground, for insulation, and easier to defend. Or to hide: for all we know, it's *completely* hidden."

"That's possible," Takenaga said. "You heard the stories about Planitia Four? No? Story goes that it was a secret underground base on Mars, built by the Americans a hundred years ago. Staffed by a team of ten people, all sworn to ultimate silence. Whatever they were doing there was so secret that when the Roussom Corporation set up its first Mars settlement and chose the exact same location as Planitia Four—their computers used the same algorithm to find the best spot for sunlight-capture, bedrock solidity, storm-shelter, and so on—the staff at Planitia had no choice but to self-destruct the base and take their own lives. The whole thing was passed off as an unexpected underground cave-in."

Sloane said, "Bull. If it was *that* secret, there wouldn't even be rumours about it."

"The point is, Huygens Base might not be visible from the surface. So how are we going to know when we've found it?"

I had to admit, Takenaga had a point there. And even if their rough calculations and estimates were accurate, and even if we *could* find the place, it was still a military base. Finding it is one problem; getting inside would be something else entirely.

It wouldn't be impossible—no building is completely impenetrable—but it was going to be tough. Especially since my old friend sub-warden Martin Copus seemed to have forgotten why some of us were on Titan in the first place.

I decided that it would be best to deal with the problem now rather than when we reached the base and it was too late.

"Boss?"

Copus was sitting slumped forward in his seat. "What now, Dredd?"

"Why are we here?"

He raised his head and looked at me. "Have you not been paying attention?"

"No, I mean, *we* as in myself, Kurya and Wightman."

"Because you and Wightman are mods and you can go out into the Bronze without a suit. And Kurya's here because she was a Med-Judge and I'm not about to put Doctor Mollo's life at risk if I don't have to; plus she was training to be part of an elite strike-force before she was arrested."

Kurya said, "That is true."

I nodded. "Good. Fine. Now... *how* are we supposed to help? Wightman and I scout ahead, find an entrance? Kurya backs us up, using her skills to breach the base. So we get inside undetected, somehow, and we find Captain Harrow if she's still alive and then... what? If we come under attack, I'm not sure that I'm comfortable facing a potential shoot-out where their side is armed with military weaponry and our side is fighting back with nothing more substantial than hopes and prayers."

Copus stared at me, and even over the constant rumble of the bus's engines I could hear him dry-swallow. Under his breath he muttered, “Stomm.”

I was enjoying this too much, I admit. Slowly, but cheerfully, I asked, “Isn’t it kind of against the rules—and common sense—to equip your prisoners with guns?”

Six

Of all the moons in the solar system, only Titan has an atmosphere with a density comparable to that on Earth. In fact, the atmosphere is *denser* than Earth's. Which means, of course, that Titan is the only moon that has powerful winds. That's one of the reasons its surface looks more Earth-like than almost any other moon: the winds mean erosion. Drifting sands, storms, the constantly freezing and thawing methane lakes... they all contribute to grinding everything down, stripping the rough edges from craters and crevasses and boulders and rocks.

The moon's air is almost completely nitrogen, with the remainder being methane and hydrogen. None of which are conducive to human health... unless that human has been modified.

So under a brown, poisonous sky, Kellan Wightman and I trudged side by side over the dusty, rocky landscape. It was like walking across an eternal stony beach at sunset on an overcast winter's day.

Not that we felt the cold much. Our polymer-laced skin and artificial blood helped keep us moving in conditions that would kill an unmodified person in seconds. Our coated eyes blinked without tears, our sealed mouths and noses kept the frost from forming within our paper lungs.

My friend Donny Guildford, now long dead, once explained to me that a mod's artificial lungs don't actually *breathe* methane, as most of the mods believed. “The body needs oxygen and there’s no oxygen *in* methane. It’s CH4: four hydrogen atoms and one carbon atom. What the apparatus *is* doing is extracting water-vapour from the atmosphere and using molybdenum-sulphide to strip its hydrogen atoms. What’s left is oxygen. It’s a miniaturised version of the prison’s atmosphere processing system, except that the big machines burn the hydrogen as fuel instead of discarding it. Besides, if they could somehow have modified our lungs to breathe methane instead of oxygen, we’d suffocate when there’s no methane around, right?”

While I did understand the science, I didn’t like to think about it too much. Tucked away in some cryogenic freezer inside the prison were my original lungs and a couple of kilograms of other body parts they’d had to remove to modify me. *That’s* a much more comforting thought: that when my sentence is done, those pieces will be returned to me and the process will be reversed. I quite like the idea that my lungs are still going to be twenty years old when the rest of me is hitting forty. Well, roughly. It’s hard to be accurate about how old I really am, being a growth-accelerated clone.

Halfway up an unusually jagged hill—so steep in parts that we had to use our hands to climb—Wightman said, “Rico, suppose the base is gone.”

“How do you mean, gone?”

“I don’t mean destroyed. Let’s say that everyone’s dead, but the building is intact.”

I guessed where he was going with this, but decided to let him take me there anyway.

“That means lots of weapons lying around. Plenty of supplies too. Who says we have to go back? We could just seal it up and defend it from the inside. I’m sure Kurya would be more inclined to take our side. That’s three against four. Good odds. We might even find a ship. A military base is bound to have some sort of shuttle. We can get off this damn rock.”

And now the conversation was back on familiar territory. “And go where?”

“Back home. Where else?”

A head-sized boulder slipped under my foot, and I turned to

watch it roll and bounce its way down the hill. "Back home, to the planet that's protected by so many early-warning systems that they'd see us coming before we even left Saturn's orbit."

"Okay then, we just stay in the base."

"How is that better than the prison? At least there we know we get to go home when our time is up."

Wightman said nothing for a few minutes, then muttered a few choice swear-words. "You're not wrong."

"I know. So you're here for arson, right?"

"Mostly because of the people who died in the fires."

"Are you guilty?"

He stopped climbing and looked at me as though I'd asked him if he could count to four. "Well, *yeah*. You know that."

"So you deserve to be here, same as me. In Mega-City One I killed a citizen I'd intended to wound. Not *entirely* my mistake, but I did it. Virgil Livingstone would probably be alive now if not for me. He was a perp, but he didn't deserve to die. I broke a lot of other laws too. All with full knowledge of what I was doing and full understanding of the impact of my actions. I'm here on Titan because this is the latest stop on the path that I chose for myself. It's not a stop that I'd *wanted* to take, but it's certainly one that I knew was possible."

Close to the top, Wightman hauled himself up onto a ridge, and sat watching me do the same. He was taller than me, so the climb was a little easier for him. "You're telling me that rehabilitation works?"

"I'm saying that I knew the risks, so I can't blame anyone but myself. Except the whole *system* is wrong. Treat the citizens as though they're all potential perps, you can't complain if they act like perps."

He rose up onto his knees, then his feet, and looked towards the hill's apex. "About a hundred metres and we should have a clear view of the base. If it's even there."

He started to move on, but I put my hand on his arm. "Hold it... A secret base will be surrounded by alarm triggers."

"I know. We should watch out for booby traps too."

I shook my head. "No, probably not. One sure way to let everyone know that they're close to your secret base is to have booby traps. You don't want to confirm your existence, you want to steer people away."

There were times when I wondered how Kellan Wightman had ever made it as a Judge in the first place. Things were said to be a little more lax in Mega-City Two, but that couldn't explain how Wightman was sometimes so stunningly oblivious. It was like he had blind spots on his brain for things like tactics and empathy.

It's not that he was stupid, as such. It was more that he lacked the imagination a good Judge requires to put himself into the perp's position. Maybe that's how he'd been caught so easily.

I told Wightman to stay put and moved on, staying on hands and knees even when I reached the apex and the hill flattened out. Snake-like, I squirmed through a series of small boulders and drifts of gravel until I was able to see the land beyond.

The base was there, but it had been very effectively disguised. From directly overhead it looked like a simple plateau, and even from this angle it wasn't noticeably artificial... except for the light shining out through a ragged blast-hole in one side. With that as a starting point, I found it relatively easy to trace the edges of the building, ignoring fake boulders and dust-drifts that the manufacturers had strategically placed to help break up the outline.

Even so, it was hard to guess the size of the place. It needed a door, or a truck, or even a human body lying on the ground to lend it scale.

Softly, Wightman's voice called, "Well?"

"It's there," I replied.

"Okay. So... what next?"

I didn't have an answer for that, so I fell back on my training and started to analyse the situation.

It had been over six hours since Governor Dodge received Captain Apolla Harrow's call for help. Aside from the blast-hole, the base showed no signs of being under attack. No sentries, no equipment, no vehicles—or even vehicle tracks—outside. The warping of the metal plates at the blast-hole told me it was an internal explosion. There was very little debris ejected from the blast-hole, as far as I could see, which meant that either someone picked it up, or there had been nothing in that particular room or corridor. Unless, of course, the explosion had taken place in the room in which Captain Harrow stored her collection of rocks and dust.

That was a joke.

I heard something moving behind me and looked back to see Wightman slowly approaching, squirming with his belly to the ground as I had.

I returned my attention to the base. The light still streaming out through the blast-hole suggested that the situation was not under control: the top priority in a covert location was discretion, and that light might as well be a kilometre-high sign with a flashing message reading, *Secret Base Here!*

Wightman settled into place next to me. "Huh. Not what I was expecting, but it makes sense. Wonder what they do here?"

"We're going to have to make a decision," I said. "If this was back home, and you were still a Judge, what would you do?"

He peered down at the base for a moment. "Find a second entrance. That section is no longer airtight; they'll have sealed it off."

"That's what I'm thinking." The lack of oxygen didn't make any difference to me and Wightman, but whoever was inside the base would have isolated the compromised tunnel, maybe even welded the inner doors shut. It's a lot easier to get through an airlock door than a welded door. But an airlock door would be harder to find.

"I'd shut off the light, too, if I was in charge," Wightman said.

"So either they want someone to see it, or whoever's running things now doesn't realise."

"Or they're *unable* to shut it off." He began to squirm backwards. "We should go back to Copus, fill him in."

I'd been mentally weighing up the possibilities since Copus had shown us the holo of Captain Harrow calling for help, and I'd come to a decision. "No, I want to get closer."

"Rico, if someone hostile has taken the base, they'll see you coming."

"That's what I'm counting on."

Seven

I TOLD WIGHTMAN to go back to the bus. "Tell Copus to give me sixty minutes."

"Then what?"

"That's up to him. But I want sixty minutes to check it out for myself."

I waited for Wightman to slither back down the other side of the hill, then moved forward.

The hill was steeper on this side, but craggier, which made climbing down a little easier. I was, of course, in full view, and for the first few metres I kept expecting a searchlight, or a shouted warning, or gunfire.

I half ran, half slid down the last few metres of loose scree, then took the time to dust myself off as well as possible: it seemed to me that if anyone *was* watching, then my casual, no-hurry, no-big-deal approach might be intriguing enough to keep their fingers off their triggers.

As I neared the hole in the wall, I was finally able to get an idea of the scale of the building: the hole was as tall as me, and had been blasted in a corridor wall. A few scraps of scorched metal were half-buried in the dust around me, but far less than I'd have expected from a hole that size: the explosion had pierced the wall but not shredded it.

I picked up a fist-sized chunk. It felt solid, but it was lighter than it looked, even taking Titan's low gravity into account. A *lot* lighter.

That was when I realised something that should have been obvious from the start. In the holo message Wightman had recognised the wall panels as foamed steel, which suggested that Harrow was on a ship. But she contacted the prison through the physical comm-link: there was no way to do that without actually being inside Huygens Base.

See, you don't fly a billion kilometres to Saturn's largest moon and then spend months building a top-secret hidden base. That would be incredibly wasteful. What you do instead is fly to the moon, land your ship and then your ship *becomes* the base. It's already airtight, it's got power, it's outfitted with crew quarters and everything else you need. Plus, in a real emergency, the whole damn thing can take off and go somewhere else.

I tossed the lump of foamed steel aside and kept walking towards the ragged opening. Now I could see the damage to the wall on the other side of the corridor, and to the floor and ceiling: the explosion had not been caused by a shaped charge.

I climbed the slight incline leading to the hole and this close it was even more obvious that this was no natural plateau. The exterior hull of the ship had been copiously but inexpertly sprayed with a plastic paint that was a reasonable match for the surrounding dirt, and many of the "plateau's" larger boulders and outcrops were clearly fake. They were covered with seam-lines and fingerprints, and here and there the wire-mesh framework showed through.

Once, in Mega-City One, I investigated the death of an actor on a set modelled on twentieth-century Detroit, and that set was what the half-buried ship reminded me of. From a distance, it was the perfect illusion; but up close it was a mess.

As I stepped inside, normal gravity returned—or close to normal, anyway—and I sniffed the air. My cybernetic olfactory system wasn't particularly well-calibrated, but I could still detect scorched metal and plastic.

Inside, the corridor seemed empty. To the right, it stretched on for about ten metres before curving away, and to the left, a few steps away, was a sealed interior door.

I walked up to the door and knocked on it.

My logic, which seemed sound at the time, was this: if someone hostile had taken control of the base, then they'd probably assume that a prisoner would be on their side. But if Captain Harrow or one of her people had regained control, then they were the ones who'd called for help. So either way, whoever was in charge would be pleased to see me.

Or, at least, not overtly hostile.

Wightman's idea of finding a second way in, on the grounds that any internal doors close to the rupture would have been sealed, seemed less likely now that I knew that this was a starship. Every internal door on a ship—especially a military vessel—has to be completely airtight.

I knocked again, much harder, and shouted, "Open up!" in the best Judge voice I was still able to muster.

I mentally pictured a bunch of low-rank soldiers on the other side of the door wondering what to do next. If there was anyone there at all.

Could be they're all *dead*, I said to myself.

I hadn't really entertained that thought until now, and that bothered me. I had been on Titan three times as long as I'd been a Judge: maybe I was starting to lose my edge. Certainly, back in the Meg, this situation would never have lasted this long.

I was about to knock for the third time when a voice said, "Identify yourself!" It wasn't Captain Harrow, but whoever she was, she was standing on the other side of the door.

I called back, "Rico Dredd. Prisoner in the Titan mining colony."

There was an awkward silence, then the woman asked, "You armed?"

"No."

"Alone?"

"Right now, yes. But there are others waiting."

Another pause. "Former Judge?"

I nodded, then realised she couldn't see me. "That's right. From Mega-City One."

"Wait there. I need to seal off this corridor before I can open the door. Two minutes."

"Understood."

As I waited, I thought about what she'd said: "*I* need to seal off this corridor." A strong indicator that she was alone. Everyone else dead. Did that mean that she was the killer, or the survivor?

Some mechanism inside the walls clunked and rattled into life. I pictured gears grinding together and a vacuum pump drawing the air out of the corridor. After just about two minutes, as promised, the door in front of me split vertically down the centre and slid neatly and near-silently into the walls.

Inside, the short corridor seemed clean and safe. Another door at the far end, ten metres away, and two more set into the right wall, about four metres apart. No debris, bullet-holes, scorch marks or body parts. That was a good sign.

I stepped in, and the first door closed behind me.

There was more clunking and rattling as the air returned, then the woman's voice said, "I'm coming out now. I'm armed. I want to see you standing with your forehead pressed against the door you entered through, hands visible at all times. Try anything else and you're dead. Do you understand and acknowledge?"

"I do."

I turned around, pressed my forehead against the cold metal of the door, and stretched out my arms, fingers splayed.

Another door opened behind me, and quiet footsteps approached.

"Don't move. Don't even *twitch*."

Something warm and metallic was pressed into the small of my back, felt like the muzzle of a large-calibre rifle. A black-gloved hand quickly and expertly patted me down, then I heard her move away.

"All right. Turn around. Slowly."

I turned. Looking back at me along the barrel of a rifle was a woman in her mid-twenties.

She was a redhead; I liked that. Rich brown skin, strong build, short—barely up to my shoulder—and she was looking me square in the eye without flinching. I liked that even more.

"First Lieutenant Salome Vine. You?"

"I told you already. Rico Dredd. Former Judge, currently a prisoner at the iridium mine."

"The hell are you doing here, Dredd?"

"We got a call from Captain Harrow. There's an emergency line between here and the mine."

"And they sent you, an unarmed prisoner, into an unknown but certainly hostile situation?"

I shrugged. "I'm more expendable than a guard, and I can operate outside without an environment suit."

Vine lowered her weapon, and I got my first clear look at her face.

I'd met my share of attractive women back in the Big Meg, as a cadet and then as a Judge. Particularly as a Judge: women just gravitated towards me. And it wasn't just my looks; they weren't *that* superficial. I was physically identical to my brother and women generally steered away from him. Well, there were a few exceptions, but then the human race is peppered with crazies.

Women liked confidence, that was what I learned pretty shortly after puberty. Not arrogance, that's a different thing entirely. Confidence is when you know you'll be able to take care of something. Arrogance is when you think you're the *only* one who can take care of it.

I'd been the best Cadet in the Academy of Law and I knew it, but that wasn't arrogance, because everyone else knew it too. And I didn't dangle it over people's heads. I'm not a jerk. You don't point out your successes and tell others, "You're never gonna get there." What you do instead is tell them, "Yeah, this is me up here on top. This is your goal. I *want* you to get good enough to knock me off." It's a simple equation: the harder you try, the better you'll get. Practice can only improve your game.

But you don't get to stay at the top of the heap without putting in the work, and I guess that's what brought me to Titan.

I had been the best Judge in Mega-City One, but Little Joe had been right behind me, and he'd never slacked off. Joe never took a day to just chill and watch the world go by. He devoted every spare moment to the Law. When he wasn't hitting perps, he was hitting the books.

Have to say, a couple more years and maybe he'd have caught up with me. I'm not saying I got lazy, but my self-selected lifestyle meant that I *had* to take downtime. I worked hard to shake up the system, to make it fair for *everyone*, not just the Judges, and that included the unpleasant task of letting the perps see me as one of them. I let them think I was on the take, because a corrupt Judge can get a lot closer to a mob's centre of power than a Judge like Joe, who was always as straight and to-the-point as an arrow.

So if First Lieutenant Salome Vine was masking revulsion at my appearance, then that was a little annoying. She was the first new woman I'd met since being turned into a mod. Not counting some prisoners who'd arrived since, but then none of them had been interesting enough to snag my attention.

Vine, though... she was stunning. One of those people you know you're going to remember for the rest of your life. Maybe it was her aloofness that I found enticing. After all, the best way to get someone to want something is to tell them they can't have it. That's what her demeanour was telling me.

She stepped back towards the door from which she'd emerged. "How many others are with you?"

"Six. Four guards, two prisoners. One of the other prisoners is like me. Modified."

She watched me for a second, and it was clear that she was weighing up her options. "Okay. To be frank, Dredd, I wasn't expecting anything. The next supply ship is four months away, and it's pretty clear that this station operates under the radar. We are off the books. Do you know what that means?"

"I do. You can't call for backup through the normal channels." I took a step closer. "So for now *I'm* your backup. What's the situation?"

"One hostile, one survivor."

I said, "Got it. I'm going to operate on the assumption that you're the survivor." That was meant to be a moment of levity, but Vine didn't crack a smile. "So what happened?"

"Follow me."

She lowered her gun completely, and as she led me through the ship she filled in some of the background about the operation. "The hostile is Corporal John Armando. Thirty years old. Exceptionally skilled at hand-to-hand combat, weapons, tactics, anything you can name. Right now, he's sealed in the lower levels—but he's smart. He'll find a way through."

"What's he got down there?"

"Enough air, water and food to last five years, minimum.

More ammunition than he'll ever need. Armoury, machine room, electronics lab, hydroponics... And access to the reactor."

"You're saying that he could just destroy the base?"

"The reactor is powerful enough to knock the whole damn *moon* out of orbit. But that won't happen. There's a lot of fail-safes, and Armando doesn't have the clearance to bypass them. Or the skills to hack the computers."

"You can't just seal him in and leave him there?"

She slowed to a stop, and turned to face me. This close, I could smell her skin even with my altered olfactory system.

She looked as though she was about to say something, but frowned instead as she peered at me. Then she said, "I *know* you. I mean, I've seen you before."

"Maybe you've met my brother back in the Meg. Last I heard he's still a Judge."

"Unlikely. It's been four years since I last set foot in Mega-City One. It's your eyes. Something about them."

I guessed where she recognised me from, of course, but I preferred people to work it out for themselves. Kept at least one part of their brain busy. It had come in useful a couple of times when I was a Judge.

See, everyone was used to seeing pics of Chief Judge Eustace Fargo as an older guy. They recognise something of him in me and Little Joe, but they're not always able to place it.

But I was wrong about Vine. She leaned even closer—I swear to Grud, for a second I thought she was going to kiss me—and said, "It's you. The dead man."

"The what?"

"You're the one who survived that storm a few years back. It was my team who found you out in the Bronze, on the edge of suffocation. You were so far gone we almost didn't bother trying to resuscitate you." She stepped back, slowly shaking her head. "After everything you went through out there... What the hell did you do to end up like *this*?"

"Long story."

She nodded and resumed walking.

But before she turned away, I saw another look in her eyes. I'd seen it before, a couple of times, when I was on the streets of the

Meg. Sometimes a Judge just *knows* everything has turned a corner and there's no way back.

Vine had that look now.

Eight

THE CLOSER WE came to the engine room, the more damage I could see. First the stink of cordite and thermite in the air, then fresh bullet-scratches in the walls. Blood spray across a glass door. A discarded ammo magazine on the floor. A first-aid box smashed open, its pills and bandages scattered like confetti after a particularly brutal wedding.

Through a synthiglass panel in a closed door, a boot on the floor with a small trickle of blood streaming past. No way to tell whether the boot was occupied.

More blood-spatter, running thickly down the wall—pooling at the ground around little tooth-and-bone islands.

"How many down?" I asked Vine.

"Thirty-four."

I didn't respond to that. On the bus we'd calculated that we were sending the base enough food for eighty people, roughly. What were they doing with the rest of it?

And then a picture of Kellan Wightman's stash of fermenting fruit and vegetables jumped into my mind. That made sense. These people were soldiers, not prisoners. They probably had their own still somewhere on the base, and I was sure it would be more elaborate and more efficient than Wightman's collection of hidden barrels.

"So what is it that you do here?"

"That's classified," Vine said. I got the feeling that it was such an automatic response that she didn't register either the question or the answer.

She glanced back at me. "I know everything's fubar now, but that doesn't change the meaning of the word 'covert.' A former Judge should understand that."

"I do. But—"

"If and when you need to know, I'll tell you." No nonsense, to-the-point. I was liking her more by the minute.

Ahead, the corridor split, with a staircase on the right. Vine didn't say anything, but she'd slowed a little, her movements becoming more cautious, more deliberate.

"We're close?" I asked, as softly as my voicebox would allow.

She nodded. "He's down there."

We stopped at the top of the staircase and she hunkered down, then motioned for me to do the same.

Below, I could see yet another sealed door—this one cutting off a smeared trail of blood. Something had been dragged through: going from the crimson fingerprints low on the door frame, a person. One who, at the time, was still alive.

Vine said, "I've sealed every door out of there but that one."

"Makes sense," I said. "Leave Armando an obvious way out. If he's as smart as you say, he'll know it's a trap and won't take it. Which means that's our way *in.*" I stood up again. "All right. Eight of us should be enough to take him down."

She sighed. "Typical Judge. Ego the size of Jupiter. Dredd, Armando killed thirty-four highly-trained marines in the space of eighteen minutes, most of them with his bare hands. The only reason I survived was because I was out on the surface at the time."

I ignored that. "Can you patch into the base's internal cameras? See where he is right now?"

Vine lifted up her left arm, showing me the small datapad attached to her wrist. It was displaying a map with a slowly-flashing dot in the centre. "That's him. About twelve metres along on the other side of that door." She raised her wrist to her mouth and softly said, "Computer. Best visual on Corporal John Armando."

The datapad's screen switched to a security camera feed.

Armando was barefoot, and naked from the waist up; he had a large, well-defined build. He was standing perfectly still with his arms by his sides and his eyes closed. His chest rose and fell regularly and deeply. What I at first took to be an aberration of the camera lens or the screen was clarified when it switched to a different angle. Armando's skin was as grey as mine.

"Something you're not telling me?" I asked.

"There's a *lot* I'm not telling you."

"Can you open the door remotely? See how he reacts?"

"We tried that shortly before you showed up. He just stands there. Look." She tapped at the datapad for a second, and the image pulled back. On the edge of the screen were two very clearly dead bodies: human heads are just not designed to be at that angle. "Master Sergeant Wegryn and Second Lieutenant Matheson. They'd been outside with me. We saw Armando like this, and Wegryn approached. The corporal was totally unresponsive. He looked catatonic. But when Wegryn came within two metres, Armando struck. Matheson opened fire but..." She shrugged. "I'm not saying that Armando *dodged* the rounds, but I know how good a shot Matheson was. She could hit a running target between the eyes from two hundred metres."

I pulled the datapad off her arm—she didn't protest—and poked at the screen until I found the map again. "Straight line of sight between him and the door." I began to walk down the steps. "Vine, how about you give me a gun, open the door and I shoot him?"

"We *can't* kill him. Matheson shouldn't have even tried."

"Do you mean we can't, or we aren't permitted to?"

"We're not permitted."

"Why not?"

"That's classified."

"Of course it is." I'd reached the door, so I turned back towards the lieutenant. "How close did you say the Master Sergeant got to him? Two metres?"

"Dredd, he'll kill you just as quickly as he killed everyone else."

I couldn't help smiling at that. She really didn't know who I was. "I'll take the chance. I'm clearly not a soldier, so he might not register me as hostile. Otherwise, what do we do? Wait for him to snap out of whatever trance he's in and decide to blow the reactor?"

"I told you, he can't do that," Vine said, following me down the stairs.

I handed the datapad back to her. "Keep the door open wide enough for me to get back through if I have to. And have your gun ready."

"Dredd, your life is worth less than his."

I gave her another smile. "Maybe. But is *yours?*"

"Yes, it is. And stop being so drokkin' smug, will you? You haven't seen him in action yet."

I almost said, "And you haven't seen *me* in action," but then I realised that would probably come across as even more smug. Instead, I said, "Open the door and start recording the camera feed. At the very least, if he kills me, then you can show the footage to sub-warden Copus and the others, give them some idea of what they'll be facing."

She said, "All right. If he kills you, you have the consolation that you'll be immortalised in a special how-not-to-do-it training film." Vine tapped at the datapad again, and immediately raised her rifle.

The door in front of me slid open, and a rush of warm air washed over us, carrying with it faint traces of blood, vomit and faeces.

I stepped through, very much aware of the thick smear of blood across the floor that led to a stomachless young soldier lying face up, his mouth and eyes open but unmoving.

Five metres from Armando, I stopped. He hadn't noticed me, or if he had, he was keeping a very tight rein on his reactions. I'm no shrink, but that was a level of control I wouldn't normally attribute to a frenzied killer.

Softly, I said, "Soldier...?"

No reaction.

"Corporal Armando, my name is Rico Dredd. Can you hear me?"

Still nothing.

"Corporal, I'm not your enemy. I'm unarmed. I want you to tell me what happened here, and why. Can you do that?"

He didn't respond, so I took another step, and the grey-skinned man opened his eyes, looked straight at me. But that was it. No twitching of limbs or shifting of his weight. His eyes didn't even follow me as I continued to move.

Keeping my distance, I walked slowly around him. His skin was almost the same shade as mine, and like mine was pockmarked with scars and needle marks where the cold-resistant polymers had been injected between the epidermis and the dermis.

"Corporal... John. I don't know what they did to you, but I'm guessing that it was very similar to what happened to me. Look at my arms, at my face... Can you see, John? We're the same. We're in this together. We can help each other, *protect* each other."

Though barefoot, Armando was a little taller than me. His muscles were as perfectly defined as I'd ever seen, not an ounce of unnecessary body fat. He was also completely hairless.

"I'm not a soldier," I said. "But back on Earth I was a Judge. A good one too. I knew my duty. *Semper Fidelis*. Always faithful."

Clearly, the man was in some sort of trance. Resting to conserve energy, but still on high alert. Soldier's fugue, I'd heard it called.

"John, you're not giving me a lot to work with here. This is a mess, and if we're going to sort it out, I'll need your help."

I'm nothing if not adventurous. Now directly behind him, I took another step closer.

I knew that was a mistake before my foot had even touched the ground.

Armando whirled around, lashing out with his fist. The back-handed blow struck me square in the jaw, hard enough to almost knock me off my feet.

I barely registered the hit when his powerful fist slammed into the side of my head, staggering me, a half-second before his knee caught me in the solar plexus.

But it's not so easy to knock the wind out of someone with an artificial respiratory system: I recovered almost immediately and threw myself to the side, ducking under the third blow. That left his own midriff unguarded, and I didn't waste the opportunity. I hit him hard in the stomach with my fist clenched with the ring-finger knuckle prominent: a very specialised move that some of the perps in Mega-City One referred to as the 'Judges' Incentive.' I've used it to bring down perps—and fellow prisoners—twice my weight.

Armando staggered back, but didn't fall. That was impressive. He launched himself at me again, left fist clenched and his right hand clawed. That didn't look like any kind of move I'd seen before, but I wasn't taking any more chances: I stepped back and to the side at the last moment and managed to grab his left wrist, then turned my movement into a spin, pulling him off balance.

That put me in the position to jab my left heel into the back of his knee and pull harder on his arm at the same time.

Wordlessly, he went down, and for a moment I thought that was it, I'd beaten him.

But he twisted around as he fell, locked his hand onto my wrist and suddenly he was dragging *me* off balance. I tried to pull out of it, but he continued to twist, until somehow I was on the ground, on my back. He had his right hand on my throat and his left fist pulled back.

That was when Vine lashed out towards the back of Armando's head with the butt of her rifle.

But the blow never connected. The grey man saw or sensed it coming—maybe there was a shadow, or he felt the breeze or something—and let go of me long enough to push himself up and back. The butt of the rifle slammed into Armando's back between his shoulder blades, and he reached over his head with his right hand and grabbed it, jerked it free of Vine's grip.

He kicked back at her, catching her square in the stomach: had she not been wearing body armour, that kick alone would have killed her.

He didn't even look to see how effective it had been. Instead, he immediately dropped back into position, again grabbing for my throat with his left hand as he spun the rifle around in his right. By the time his fingers locked around my neck again, he had the rifle aimed at my face with his finger on the trigger.

I had an instant where I told myself "The safety's still on!" but I couldn't take that chance. I grabbed the barrel with my left hand and pushed it aside just as he fired. The gun boomed and the muzzle-flash scorched my cheek, and later I found fragments of the foam-steel floor embedded in my skin.

Still holding onto the barrel, I shoved the rifle back towards him, trying to twist it out of his grip, and at the same time he was squeezing my throat with his free hand. If I'd been a normal man, I might have already passed out from pain or lack of oxygen, but I'm no longer a normal man. My polymer-laced skin and modified respiratory system make my throat a lot more resilient than most people's.

I slammed my right fist into his stomach over and over, as Armando fired four more times—each shot another deafening boom—and it was clear that strength-wise we were very closely matched.

I knew a little about military training, what they put the recruits through. It was intense; the system turned men and women into fighting machines, honed almost to perfection. Almost.

But I'd had fifteen years in the toughest academy on Earth. And for each of those fifteen years I'd excelled. Top of the class. Sure, Armando probably had ten more years' experience than I did, but I'd bet my time in the Mega-City One Academy of Law and my one year on the streets against anything he had.

I went for his eyes.

Now, that's a move that a rookie might make when he's desperate. You go for your enemy's eyes, you're not playing around anymore. As Wightman had said earlier, there's no going back from that. Most people are squeamish about something as harmless as eye drops; even the *thought* that an opponent might attempt to tear out their eyes is enough to send them into an absolute frenzy.

So a seasoned fighter learns not to do that. Eyes are off limits. Unless, of course, you know what you're doing. Could be that there's a time when you *want* your opponent to go into a frenzy.

That's what I did. It was a calculated risk, but it paid off.

I pressed the fingers of my right hand into a point and jabbed straight at his left eye.

Armando flinched to the side, shifting his weight and loosening his grip on my neck. That gave me the leverage I needed. I dropped my hand a little mid-strike, and instead hit him just below his jaw, driving my fingers into the carotid sinus and cracking the heel of my hand against his left clavicle, snapping it. Two points of pain with one blow.

He threw himself backwards away from me, but I was still holding onto the barrel of his rifle. I twisted my arm away, pulling him further off balance and weakening his grip on the gun, giving myself enough room to pull my right leg up and kick out.

The sole of my boot mashed satisfyingly into Armando's face, and he toppled backwards. Have to hand it to whoever trained him, they did a pretty good job: he almost recovered before I was on my feet. Almost.

I stamped down on his broken clavicle to further disorient him, then as he was silently screaming, a quick, hard kick to his left temple put him out. It felt like kicking a breezeblock, but it worked.

I pulled the rifle from his grip, spun it around and quickly checked the breech. It was clear. I held it aimed at Armando, finger off the trigger but nearby, ready.

"Drop it!" Vine shouted from behind me. "I said, drop the weapon, Dredd!"

"You *kidding* me?" I'm not ashamed to admit that the weight of the gun was both comforting and empowering, but I shook off the feeling—this wasn't the right time. "Vine, you should cuff this drokker while you have the chance."

For the second time that day, I felt the muzzle of a handgun poke into the small of my back, and Vine said, "Last warning. Drop the gun."

I opened my hand and let the rifle fall to the floor, then stepped back from it. "Cuff him. He's actually unconscious now, not just in standby mode or whatever he was before."

She passed me a set of cuffs. "You do it."

I rolled Armando onto his side and cuffed his wrists behind his back. "Give me another set. *Two* more sets, if you've got them."

"He's not superhuman, Dredd. Those cuffs are a titanium-based polymer. They're unbreakable."

"It's your funeral. Along with all your former colleagues." As I stood up, I added, "You didn't have to pull your gun on me, Vine."

"You're a prisoner. Said so yourself. I can't let you have a gun."

I straightened up, and gave her my best tight-lipped smile. Like there was any other kind of smile I could give. "This creep killed thirty-four highly-trained and heavily-armed marines, and I took him down on my own and with my bare hands. You really think I need a gun to be dangerous?"

Nine

VINE USED HER datapad to patch the base's comms system to open a short-range radio link with the prison bus, and we waited for Copus and the others to arrive. Vine told them exactly where to find us: she didn't want to leave Armando alone, and certainly didn't trust me on my own.

I sat on the floor with my back to the wall, watching the grey-skinned corporal. "So what *is* this? You're experimenting on soldiers here?"

Vine was looking at her datapad as she lowered herself down close to me. "Dredd... You should have died out there in the Bronze, but you're made of strong stuff. I've just pulled your records. I know who you were before your sentencing." She tapped at the screen. "You were already exceptional, and *now* look at you. I knew about the modification process when I was assigned to this base, but this is the first time I've seen the results in person..." She hesitated for a few seconds, and it was clear to me that she was debating whether to carry on or just end this conversation right here and now. "No, that's not true. Out in the Bronze, shortly after we found you... We recovered a body. He'd been modified just like you."

My artificial skin crawled at that. "Guildford," I said. "Donny Guildford. He was a friend."

"I'm sorry to hear that. He'd been shot in the head."

"I know." At night, sometimes, I could still hear the echo of that gunshot. I mentally shook myself. This wasn't the time. "So your people examined Guildford's body. Reverse-engineered the process. And now you've done the same to Corporal Armando. To his skin, at least."

"Correct. He..." Again, she faltered. "He clearly didn't take to it as well as you have. We haven't done any work on his lungs or other organs yet, just his skin and eyes. We chose Corporal Armando because physically he was the strongest of all the candidates. Most of the time he's more or less normal, but I know he has nightmares. I think we broken him." She turned to look at me. "How did you come out of the process intact, Dredd?"

"I don't know the details," I told her. "And I don't really *want* to know. They wiped my memory of the procedure. Not entirely—I still get flashes from time to time—but enough that I can't actually recall it. It keeps slipping away, like a dream I can *almost* remember. Lieutenant, are you telling me that your people subjected Corporal Armando to the process *without* suppressing his memories?"

She didn't answer. Instead, she said, "He wasn't a volunteer, Dredd. Seventeen months ago he was stationed on JupSat and got into a brawl with an officer. We don't know the exact circumstances of the disagreement—a lot of the information has been redacted—but the officer didn't survive. Armando was court-martialled and sentenced to forty years. He was offered a reduction in sentence if he participated in this programme."

I leaned my head back against the wall, pretty sure I knew where this was going. "You just said he *wasn't* a volunteer."

"Captain Harrow decided that he was the best fit of all the candidates by some distance."

I swear, if I'd still been a Judge, I'd have arrested her there and then. As it was, I felt sick. Whatever people have said about me, they know I'm not a sadist. I don't get off on people being hurt against their will.

Harrow and her engineers had subjected Armando to unimaginable agony. Was it any wonder that his mind had fractured?

Vine said, "I'm not cleared to know everything they did to him. But something inside him snapped this morning. He shared quarters with Second Lieutenants Baily-White and Underwood, and Doctor Riahi, his handler. And today, before first shift, Armando just went berserk. I saw the CCTV footage: it's dark, hard to see much more than just a triangle of light coming in through the open door. They're in their bunks, Riahi's on her side, facing Armando. She says something to him, and he grabs his sidearm and starts shooting. Two in the head and one in the chest for Riahi, same for the others. And then he came for the rest of us."

"So what was it that Riahi told him?"

A shrug. "Unknown. The audio quality is poor, and she was speaking softly so as not to waken the others. She and Armando were friends; they would often spend hours at night talking, especially when he was finding it hard to sleep."

"You were outside when it happened?"

"Yeah. With Master Sergeant Wegryn and Second Lieutenant Matheson, checking the perimeter sensors." She tilted her head back, looking upwards. "Near as I can tell, the damage to the hull was caused by a sack of blastbombs—shrapnel-less grenades. They were trying to trap Armando in that section. It's the longest run of corridor with an exterior wall. Clearly, they mistimed it. But it was the explosion that drew our attention."

"No radio alert?"

She raised an eyebrow. "Covert ops, Dredd. Emphasis on 'covert.' Radio signals would be something of a giveaway. We do have an emergency link to... let's just say it's another base. I guess Captain Harrow must have figured that she was more likely to get a faster response from the prison than from Colonel D'Angelo."

"Who's that?"

"In charge of this entire operation. He and his elite guard are off-base right now: he has a lot of other projects to oversee."

"So what now?"

Vine shrugged. "Good question. I guess I'm the acting CO until the Colonel makes contact—we have no way to contact *him*—but that could be weeks, even months. I can't stay here with only the corporal for company."

* * *

Sub-warden Copus stood in the doorway and looked from me to First Lieutenant Vine to the still-unconscious Corporal Armando, and then back to me. "What the hell, Dredd?"

As Kurya tended to Vine's and Armando's injuries, I explained the situation to Copus, then said, "Either we station some people out here until Colonel D'Angelo makes contact, or we bring them back with us."

McConnach said, "Sir, that could work out all right. Word will already have spread throughout the prison about the out-of-control freighter. We just need to brief Vine and keep Armando sedated, tell everyone that they're survivors of the crash."

Again, Copus looked towards Armando. "And his skin-colour? How do we explain that?"

"Asteroid miner," I said. "We say that they used the same process that we do here. Except that it's voluntary."

McConnach nodded. "Yeah, that's good. And that explains how he survived the crash intact. Extra-tough skin. Vine survived because he shielded her. Makes him a hero. People are less inclined to question heroes."

I didn't agree with that, but this wasn't the time for that argument.

Copus absently chewed on his lower lip for a few seconds, then said, "Drokk it. We have no choice. Standard maritime laws still apply out here—you have to offer help to anyone in distress. But if that psycho gets loose and freaks out, I'm going to put a round between his ears, don't care how much the military want to hide him."

"That's the right call," I said.

Copus turned away. "I don't need your approval or consent, Dredd. You, Wightman and Kurya stay put."

McConnach and Sloane stood guard while Copus and Takenaga coordinated with Vine on the process of checking the base room by room, level by level, locking every door as the rooms were cleared. They had to account for every corpse, every weapon. They left the bodies where they found them—there'd be an investigation at some stage—but they logged and tagged them.

Wightman and I were tasked with carrying Armando back up to the entrance, then everyone took part in a lengthy discussion on how to transport the unconscious Corporal Armando from the base to the bus. With his hands cuffed there was no way we could put him into an environment suit—and it's already hard enough putting a suit on someone unconscious: for a start, it takes forever just to get their fingers into the gloves—so in the end we just put a helmet on him, used strips of environment suit puncture-tape to seal the edges around his neck, rested an oxygen tank on his chest, and carried him out on a stretcher.

Getting him through the bus's airlock was even more tricky, because it can really only take one person at time. Puncture-tape came in handy again: we used it to secure him upright to the inner wall of the airlock—I say "we," but it was mostly me. It wasn't easy with so little room in which to work. When I was sure he wasn't going to topple forward, I left him there, closed the outer door, then watched as the inner door opened and McConnach and Sloane peeled the tape free and carried him inside.

Then Kurya, Wightman and I were each frisked and scanned twice before we were allowed back onto the bus.

I took a last look at the base as we rolled away, but Vine had shut off the corridor light and now all that I could see was a rocky plateau.

The journey back was a little slower, but more direct: no one cared any more about hiding our path.

Along the way, Copus and Vine conversed with a brow-creasing intensity, their voices too low for me to overhear. Takenaga slept, while McConnach and Kurya kept watch on Armando, who was stretched out across the back seat, still unconscious.

Wightman sat in the seat in front of me, with his back to the side window so that he could keep an eye on everyone else. "Thirty-*four?*" he asked.

I nodded.

"Damn. Why the hell didn't Vine just put the drokker down?"

"She won't say."

"Maybe he's bullet-proof?"

"Could be, but I doubt it."

Wightman started patting his pockets. "You hungry?"

I realised that I was. "Haven't eaten since breakfast."

"It's on me." He hauled himself out of his seat and made his way to the storage lockers, then came back with four medium-sized tubes of food-paste. "What do you feel like, Rico? We've got... Vegetable Stew, Mock Chicken Dinner, All-Feast, or Supplementary."

"Like it makes one damn bit of difference." I held out my hand and he slapped the Vegetable Stew and Supplementary tubes into it.

I missed food more than anything else. Real, proper actual food that you could taste and chew. When they modify your body to survive on Titan, they don't just reinforce your skin and replace your lungs: part of the process involves sealing up your mouth and nose. They cut a hole in your throat and fit a voicebox, and it's through that hole that you eat and drink.

Upside: you no longer have to brush your teeth.

Downside: everything else. You can't taste much any more. You have to re-learn how to talk. You spend the first couple of months genuinely worried that you might drown in your own saliva. You can't even properly kiss someone. Can't whistle, either, though that's less of a big deal.

By now I was used to feeding myself through the voicebox, but I was still a little self-conscious about it. I didn't like anyone watching at me as I did it.

Wightman had no such restrictions. He popped out the voicebox and held it in his left hand while he squirted the entire contents of the Mock Chicken Dinner through the hole in one go. Then he sat back and pretended to dab at the corners of his mouth with a handkerchief. "Ah... bland, unsatisfying and soul-destroying, just how I like it. My lack of compliments to the chef."

I consumed half of the Supplementary tube—a brown paste supposedly laced with all the minerals and vitamins a person might need in one day—and tried not to think about a large bowl of macaroni and cheese.

There's a story that gets passed on from one mod to another about the very first guy to get the treatment, back on Enceladus. Apparently he starved to death because he just couldn't keep the food down. Could be true. There were times when I thought I really couldn't face another meal squeezed from a damn tube, but I knew that the only sane approach was to get it over with and try to think of something else.

For any prisoner, in the early days of the sentence, a good distraction is to try to calculate the number of days you have left. But pretty soon you've worked it out exactly, and confirmed it by doing it again a few times, and after that you just subtract another day each morning.

In my spare moments, or when things were particularly tough, I would often think of my patrol routes in Mega-City One, try to recall every side-street, every store, every block. It wasn't easy, and on a couple of occasions I got stuck on a name and that was maddening—I once had to ask sub-warden Giambalvo to look up a map of the city and tell me the name of the block between Sal Schoeppner Apartments and Kenji Mizoguchi Block, because I was sure I'd end up with an aneurysm trying to remember it. I chose Giambalvo because I knew she'd worked in the same sector. She told me to take a hike, but the next day she stopped me in the corridor and said, "You drokker, Dredd. You had me awake all night wondering about that. I had to get up and check it out. Windward Ranch Habitats."

I was just squeezing out the last of the Vegetable Stew paste when Copus shouted for everyone's attention.

"This is the story we're... You *listening*, Kurya? This is the story we're going to tell when we get back to the mine. Do not discuss the real situation even amongst yourselves, understood? Four days ago the freighter *Carol Masters* was en route to Mimas when a power-coupling blew in the engine core. The crew had no choice but to detach the core and use the thrusters to steer towards Titan. They were able to slow a little so that they didn't completely break up in the atmosphere, but they hit hard. It came down four kilometres south of Brunel's Ridge. All hands lost with the exception of Petty Officer Salome Vine and engineer John Armando. In this version of the truth, Armando is a former asteroid miner who voluntarily underwent the same skin-reinforcing procedure as Wightman and Dredd and the other mods. He suffered a serious concussion in the crash and has been reacting with extreme hostility, hence the need for the cuffs. Any questions?"

Takenaga asked, "Why concoct a story at all? We place them both in crew quarters. If we dock at the south entrance, we can go straight through to Admin without encountering any other prisoners."

"Because the chances are they're going to be with us for four months, until the next Earth ship comes."

Vine said, "That's unless my superiors decide to check on Huygens Base, in which case they'll get no answer and come looking. We operated with almost complete autonomy, so there are no visits scheduled, and surprise inspections don't happen this far out."

"Yeah, but what did you actually *do* there?" Wightman asked.

"That's classified."

Copus added, "And it's none of your damn business anyway, Wightman. Are we all clear on the story?"

I looked around at the others. They seemed to be satisfied, but I wasn't. I said, "What was the freighter carrying to Mimas?"

He hesitated long enough for me to know that they hadn't thought that far ahead. "Doesn't matter."

I said, "Tectonic surveillance equipment that's too delicate to launch on its own, and has to be set up and calibrated by hand. The expert in question was Professor... Paxton. Ilia Paxton. Female, forty years old, two kids. She didn't want to be there, but she was the only one qualified."

Copus raised his eyes. "You're overpainting this picture, Rico. No one is going to ask."

"Four months," I reminded him. "Boss, when a new guard arrives at the prison, we all know everything about them by the end of their first *week*."

McConnach said, "He's right about that. What type of ship was the freighter? How many crew? Captain's name? Where was it coming from? You said it didn't completely break up in the atmosphere, so what parts of it did? Was the hull breached and *that's* how everyone died? How come Vine and Armando came out completely intact? Maybe there was a couple of others who survived the impact, but they died before we got to them. We can build on that, too, if we say that there was a crevasse or something in the way and we had to go around it, but if we hadn't, then we would have got there sooner and maybe we could have saved one of the others. Then..." She trailed off as she realised everyone was staring at her. "Sorry."

I said, "Don't be. Most of us trained to be Judges. We were taught how to spot the holes in fake alibis. And so were at least half of the other prisoners. Consistency and solidity is the key to credibility."

Zera Kurya said, "You are all wrong. We tell the other prisoners and guards that it was a crashed covert military vessel. We give them no further answers because we *know* no further answers."

I didn't want to admit it in front of the others, but she was right. Keep the story as close to the truth as possible.

One by one we drifted off to sleep. The last thing I remember was Sloane singing "The Ballad of Skrimpy Doodle" to himself as he drove. He was getting the words wrong, but I didn't correct him. He looked happy and there wasn't a lot of that to be found on Titan.

Ten

THE BUS SCREECHED and hissed and clunked to a stop and I was awake before the final judder of its brakes.

Sloane was saying, "Mister Copus...? Oh, drokk... someone wake up Copus." He turned back and yelled, "*Now*, drokk it!"

The sub-warden had been stretched out across two seats. He rolled to his feet and started to haul himself towards the front. "What? What is it?"

First Lieutenant Vine was already standing next to Sloane, looking out through the windscreen. "It's a ship. An Omicron-Twelve. About two hundred metres dead ahead."

Sloane said, "It just set down. Flew straight overhead, hovered for a bit, then set down."

"Check the radio," Vine said, checking the datapad fixed to her wrist. "Scan bands two, four and five if you don't get an immediate signal."

I was in the process of getting out of my seat when Giambalvo said, "Stay put, Dredd. All of you."

Copus asked Vine, "Anything?"

She nodded. "Just come in... It's Colonel D'Angelo. They picked up my call from the base to this bus. We're to hold position until further notice."

Sloane turned around to face Copus, "Nothing on the air, sir.

Can't even get a link to the mine."

Vine said, "They'll be jamming everything. We might as well get comfortable. Could be a while before they decide it's safe."

Kurya, Wightman and I settled back. We were prisoners; we were used to being trapped in a small space with nothing to do. And Vine seemed calm enough too. It was the guards who would crack first.

It was almost an hour before Vine's datapad beeped again. She showed the message to Copus and he nodded slowly before turning around to the rest of us.

"Need a volunteer. Dredd, that's you."

I pulled myself to my feet. "I swear, when I get home, first thing I'm going to do is send a dictionary to every guard on this damn moon."

"They know we have Corporal Armando, and they want him back."

"So why am *I* the volunteer? Why not him?"

Copus said, "Walk towards their ship. You'll be met halfway by a member of the colonel's team."

"And...?"

"And that's all we know." He nodded towards the airlock. "Get moving."

I stepped into the airlock and waited for the air to be pumped out, then the outer door opened and I stepped out into the Bronze.

Humans are adaptable and can get used to anything. Occasionally I forget that I'm no longer the man I once was, and then something happens to remind me. As I emerged from the shadow of the Big Bus there was a part of me that expected to be hit by a warm breeze, and when that didn't happen I remembered that I no longer really felt the cold or the heat.

It's the little things that can crush a prisoner's spirit. Common experiences that we all take for granted until they're no longer there. Here's another one: using your teeth to tear open a candy-bar wrapper. Okay, so there's not much candy on Titan, but that's not the point: my teeth were now locked away behind sealed lips.

I glanced back at the bus to see Copus glaring at me with his usual Why-isn't-it-done-yet? expression, then returned my attention to the task at hand: walk until I meet some other person. Not the most arduous of projects.

I'd gone about fifty paces when I saw the ship. It was smaller than the bus. Even smaller than a H-Wagon back home. It looked like someone had taken a large block of metal and hollowed out the inside, stuck the biggest engines they could find on the back, a big window on the front, and an assortment of small wings at odd angles. I didn't know a lot about spacecraft, but this thing looked about as easy to fly as the average kitchen.

A hatch opened in the side and a man wearing full body armour climbed out. He looked in my direction for a second, then reached back into the craft and pulled out a large gun. My eyesight isn't the best, but even from here I recognised a fully-automatic assault rifle.

He slung the rifle onto his left shoulder, then started to stride towards me.

The closer we came, the more of his armour I could see. Close-fitting, like the armour Vine was wearing, but darker. No insignia or rank-markings. A few scratches on the shoulder-plates and chest-plate. Utility belt, with a handgun hanging from it.

His helmet was full face, of course, with an almost opaque visor. Given how poor the sunlight is on Titan, I figured he had to have light-enhancing tech inside the helmet.

We were maybe ten metres apart when the wind picked up suddenly, a brief but powerful gust. I was used to that, but this guy wasn't: he swayed a little, almost stumbled. I liked that. It humanised him.

I called out, "You'd want to watch out for that. We get a lot of weather here on Titan."

He stopped two metres in front of me, but didn't reply.

"So who are you?" I asked, looking at my own reflection in his visor.

"Identify yourself."

"Rico Eustace Dredd. Prisoner. Former Mega-City One Judge. You?"

"Sears."

"That's it?" I asked. "No other name? No rank or title?"

"Identify all persons on your transport. Names, duties, ranks."

I recognised this approach. It's one of the methods we learned during Basic Interrogation back at the Academy of Law. Abrupt, impersonal, to-the-point. It makes the suspect feel like they have no control over the situation. It often works, too, but that depends on the suspect. In some cases it triggers their defences and they clam up even tighter.

I found myself reacting that way. Part of me was thinking, *Don't tell this drokker anything!* but then I caught myself. I wasn't a suspect. I hadn't done anything wrong. Well, not in the current context.

So I told him who was on board the bus, and he just stood there. He didn't nod or react in any other way.

When I was done, he asked, "Have you or any members of your party established contact of any kind with your own HQ since you departed on this mission?"

"Not to my knowledge."

"Return to your transport. Inform your CO that you are ordered to reverse your course and return to Huygens Base."

I decided that it was my turn to be the enigmatic one. I stood still and didn't respond.

He repeated himself, a little more aggressively. "Return to your transport. Inform your CO that you are ordered to reverse your course and return to Huygens Base."

I asked, "Is that an order? Because as far as I can see, you have no rank. And even if you had, that makes not one damn iota of difference to me, because I'm not in the military. You have no authority over me."

Keeping his arms by his side, Sears shrugged his left shoulder and his assault rifle slid down his arm and into his hand. Clearly a heavily practised manoeuvre, but still impressive. And probably very unsettling if you're already nervous around people in authority.

I said, "Cheap trick. But I was a Judge—that doesn't scare me."

He regarded me silently for another couple of seconds. "You have your orders." Then he turned and started walking back towards the small craft.

I called out after him, "What if we don't comply?"

He just kept walking, so I headed back towards the bus.

Before I reached it, Sears' ship had lifted off and passed back overhead.

Back inside, I told Copus what had happened, then he, Takenaga and Vine went to a quiet corner to discuss the situation.

Me, if I'd been in command, I wouldn't have wasted that time. I'd have gone back to Huygens. Not because I felt threatened by Sears, but because I still wanted to know what they'd been doing in that place, aside from getting halfway to turning Corporal Armando into a mod.

Twice during their huddled discussion, Copus turned to me and asked, "You're *sure* he said nothing else?"

"I'm sure."

Eventually, they reached a decision. "We're going back to Huygens Base," Copus said. "Mister Sloane, start us up and turn us around."

As the engines rumbled back to life, Wightman groaned. "Aw hell. Just realised. Mister Copus, me and Rico are gonna have to purge our filters soon."

Copus grunted his annoyance. "How long can you put it off?"

"Couple of hours," I said.

"Our ETA is three hours twenty," Sloane said.

"Should be okay. If not, we can do it here in the bus."

I could see Sloane failing to suppress a shudder at that. He'd clearly been a witness to mods purging their sinus filters.

Copus said, "Hold off as long as possible."

SLOANE'S ESTIMATE OF the journey time turned out to be on the money: three hours and twenty-one minutes later, the big bus rumbled to a stop a hundred metres from the Huygens Base plateau.

Sitting in the seat behind me, Wightman muttered, "We are never getting home, are we? The marines are gonna execute us or something." His voice was thick, clogged, his breathing starting to sound sticky. I knew mine would be too, if I spoke.

A little under eight hours earlier we'd had the fun and games of carrying a cuffed, unconscious man from Huygens Base onto the bus, and now we were faced with doing the same thing again in reverse, and our supply of puncture-tape was running low. Copus, Vine and McConnach were deep in discussion as to how we were going to manage it when a man's voice from the back of the bus said, "I can walk."

I looked towards Armando. He was still lying across the back seat, facing away from us with his hands triple-cuffed behind his back.

Vine slowly approached him. "Corporal... are you lucid?"

"Is that you, Lieutenant?"

"It's me. Corporal, do you know where you are?"

He twisted around a little. "Prison transport. From what I can see of it, it looks like two old Bekka Trundlers welded together."

Sloane quietly said, "He's not wrong there."

Copus eased himself past Vine and stopped two seats away from Armando. "Corporal, my name is Martin Copus, sub-warden at the prison. You and Vine are the only two survivors of Huygens Base."

A pause, then Armando said, "I know."

Copus glanced back at us. "You know?"

"I know what happened. I remember what went down. But I wasn't in control..."

Vine asked, "Corporal, what did Doctor Riahi tell you that caused you to *lose* control?"

"I... I don't recall that. Lieutenant, permission to speak freely?"

Vine said, "Go ahead."

"I'm starving and I pretty urgently need to use the head, sir."

"Understood. Corporal, we were stopped en route to the prison by Colonel D'Angelo, who has ordered us to return to Huygens. Which is where we are now. We'll get you inside, but we're not taking off the cuffs. Not after what happened this morning."

Armando squirmed around until he was lying on his back, then swung his feet onto the floor, wedged them under the seat in front, and used them to lever himself up into a sitting position. He took a moment to look at all of us, one by one.

When his eyes locked with mine, he just nodded—acknowledgement to the one man who had beaten him—then he moved on.

Lieutenant Vine said, "All right. Let's go. Mister Copus?"

The sub-warden did his usual instruction-barking and they

donned their environment suits, then we filed off the bus, with Armando second-last—wearing just a helmet sealed with re-used strips of puncture-tape—and Vine following.

Two armour-wearing marines stood guard outside the blast hole in the wall of the fake plateau.

Copus said, "We don't know the situation. All of you keep your hands to yourselves, say nothing unless you have to. Lieutenant, lead the way."

I was about to fall in line with the others when Copus put his hand on my arm. When I glanced back at him, he was shaking his head.

He waited until the others were several metres away before nodding and gesturing for me to walk ahead of him.

"I know what you're thinking, boss," I said. "This whole situation stinks like the Resyk drains on a hot summer's day."

"Meaning?"

"If you're running a top-secret military project and something goes horribly wrong and then some civilians come in to rescue the survivors, well, it seems to me that you might get to thinking that those civilians are not part of the solution at all. They've become part of the problem."

"Yeah," he said. "That's what I figured *you* were thinking. Not me. You're a perp, Dredd, so you think like a perp and you assume everyone else does too. I agree that this is a highly-charged situation, but the one thing it does *not* need is you trying to be a hero if something goes wrong. When we get inside, you'll keep your mouth shut unless I say otherwise. Understood?"

"I won't say anything." Not because I felt intimidated by him. Hell, I *liked* Copus. He reminded me of myself in a lot of ways. No stomm, get the job done, we're not here to be friends. If more people were like us, the human race wouldn't be so screwed up.

Take your average start-up small company, for example. It might have, say, ten employees: one boss and nine workers. They all understand each other's clearly-defined roles, they know what they have to do, so they get the job done. Sure, they have some fun along the way, but each one of them knows that ultimately the work takes priority. But then the company is successful and expands. Ten years later, it's got a hundred employees. One big boss overseeing three or four department chiefs, each department divided into sub-sections, each sub-section with five or six people who have no idea what anyone else in the company does, but they're damn sure that everyone else is getting paid more than they are. And now the company's just another cluster of grumbling employees who hate their jobs and do the bare minimum of work to avoid getting fired.

That's why someone like Copus is a good leader. Chief Judge Fargo was the same. If you're doing your job, you don't have time to worry about how much your contemporaries are getting paid, and it's not important anyway.

Some of the guards were heel-dragging daydreamers. Kalai Takenaga was a bit like that. She was pleasant enough, but just didn't seem to care much about the job. When we were out on the surface scanning for iridium deposits, we always knew that she would call a halt to it and end the shift as soon as the quota was reached or the time was up. She would literally be watching the clock *and* the weight of the yield. She didn't care whether we talked or sang or told jokes, as long as the work got done, and she rarely interacted with us unless it was to correct someone who said "could of" or misused "whom."

But the other guards would often push us harder. For some of them it was a matter of personal pride that each shift finished with a higher yield than the last.

Sure, it was practically slave labour and we prisoners hated every minute of it, but that's not the point. In that example, it's not about us. It's about the guards.

Back at the Academy, Judge-Tutor Semple used to tell us, "The average person can make better music by playing the radio than by playing the piano, but it's not nearly as satisfying and it achieves nothing new. There's no pride in that."

Still, it bugged me that Copus had singled me out. I'd never given him any reason not to trust me.

Okay, it could be argued that I'd killed four wardens that time we were trapped out in the Bronze; but that had been to save my own life, and Copus didn't really know the full story.

Some of the prisoners were constantly in trouble, always fighting against the system, but that was a master-class in futility. The best way to avoid drowning is to swim *with* the flow, not against it.

So I let it go. No point in being offended because offence is like worry: it gets you nowhere and it's just one more thing to carry around with you.

Ahead, Vine and Armando passed between the two marines and in through the ragged hole, followed by McConnach, Wightman and the others.

Then it was my turn. As I set foot on the base's foamed-steel floor, a thought occurred to me and I turned around to mention it to sub-warden Copus, but the expression on his face told me to keep it to myself for now.

Eleven

ONCE WE WERE all inside the sealed-off corridor and the air had been restored, one of the marines opened an inner door and said, "Follow me. Single file."

It was the same route I'd taken earlier with Vine.

The marine walked ahead of us, and the other behind us. There was almost no way to tell them apart, not counting different notches and scratches on their armour. No insignia, no numbers, no different blocks of colour.

Wightman must have been thinking along the same lines, because as we passed a third marine standing guard outside a door, he asked, "So, your visors have a HUD that tells you who's who, right?"

He didn't respond to that, but fell into step alongside the one trailing us.

We were channelled into a large, empty room off the main corridor where a fourth marine was waiting. Again, he was wearing armour identical to the others', but I said, "A pleasure to see you again, Sears."

No reaction, but I was sure that under his helmet he'd be angry. I wasn't about to admit that I recognised a particular scratch on his left boot.

Sears said, "Remove your environment suits and leave them in this room, along with any and all weapons or electronic equipment on your person."

"I'm sub-warden Martin Copus. I want to speak to Colonel D'Angelo."

"Just do as you're instructed, sub-warden."

Wightman and I waited as the others stripped off their suits, then we were all very efficiently and thoroughly searched and frisked. That's something you get used to very quickly as a prisoner: we were frisked every time we returned from the mines or from outside. It soon gets so that if they forget about the frisking, you feel left out.

The marines spent a few moments with me and Wightman, examining our cybernetic enhancements, then they ordered us out into the corridor—I noticed that Sears locked the door as he left—and again marched us through the base.

Our path took us past the infirmary, through a narrow mess-hall, and into an empty hangar that clearly doubled as the base's gymnasium: basketball hoops had been attached to opposite walls and court-lines had been crudely spray-painted on the floor.

Sears said, "Stand in the centre of the room. You will not speak."

Sloane asked, "Why not?"

The soldier closest to him slammed him in the stomach with the butt of his rifle.

Copus jumped forward and was instantly the target of three further weapons.

Then the door opened again, and another marine entered, accompanied by a slender, slightly awkward-looking young man in a somewhat creased dress uniform: he'd clearly been wearing it under an environment suit. Watching his bearing, I concluded that this man had never seen combat.

The young man nodded to Sears, who said. "This is Colonel Peter D'Angelo."

Colonel D'Angelo said, "You will all be silent unless directed otherwise." He slowly turned to look at Copus. "Is that clear, or is a further demonstration required?"

The sub-warden nodded. "It's clear. But, look, what the drokk *is* this?"

A handgun boomed twice and everyone flinched. Copus staggered backwards, clutching his left shoulder. "Son of a..." He collapsed into a sitting position.

One of the soldiers stepped forward and pressed the muzzle of his gun right into the centre of Copus's forehead. "You heard the colonel—not one more drokkin' *word!*"

The colonel said, "Stand down, Lancaster." The soldier stepped back, leaving a scorch-mark on Copus's face where the still-hot muzzle had burned it.

The colonel said, "One of you tend to his wound."

Zera Kurya crouched down next to Copus and tore open his shirt. "Clean shot, clipped the muscle. No major damage as far as I can see." She glanced around. "Steripatch?"

One of the marines pulled a pack of steripatches from a pouch on her belt and tossed it to Kurya. She peeled off the backing from a patch, and slapped it over the wound.

Colonel D'Angelo gestured to Vine. "Come forward, First Lieutenant Vine and Corporal Armando."

Vine and Armando stepped up to him.

To Armando, he said, "You are a disappointment, soldier. A failure." The colonel's eyes narrowed as he turned to Vine. "You broke protocol, Lieutenant."

She didn't respond to that. I don't blame her; they'd just shot Copus for speaking up.

"This is a covert operation and your primary goal is to keep it that way. You invited civilians onto the base. You are hereby stripped of your rank and will be court-martialled."

D'Angelo moved away from Vine and peered at the rest of us. "Huygens Base is a highly classified facility; you were never supposed to know of its existence. This facility was established at the same time as your prison, along with a direct link connecting the base to your emergency system. That link was supposed to be used only in extreme circumstances. But Captain Harrow used that link to initiate contact with Governor Dodge eight years ago. I believe that Dodge was under the impression that said contact was sanctioned and within the purview of Harrow's mission. Harrow's personal logs show that she and Dodge had an arrangement to supply this base with fresh fruit and vegetables in return for the use of certain unspecified equipment." D'Angelo walked up to Copus and looked down at him. "What equipment?"

Copus shrugged. "This is the first I've heard about it."

"You're lying. Do so again, and the next shot will do permanent damage."

Copus used his uninjured arm to wipe a bead of sweat from his forehead. "Harrow agreed to recalibrate the base's satellite to scan the moon for iridium deposits. Our own scanners can penetrate eighty metres at most, depending on the bedrock. The satellite is much more powerful. The data she returned meant we were able to almost double our yield."

The colonel took all this in without a word. His body language was hard to read, but it seemed to me that he wasn't discovering anything he didn't already know.

He returned to Vine. "You understand what you have done, Lieutenant? The breach of security you have committed? Permission to speak."

"Sir, I—" She abruptly cut herself off, inhaled deeply through her nostrils, and stared unblinking at the slender Colonel. "Salome Pamelina Vine. Marine Corps, First Lieutenant. Serial number M-triple-zero-two-four-seven-four-zero-one."

D'Angelo frowned at her. "You will respect the chain of command, Vine. This is a critical situation and your forthcoming court-martial will not be derailed or delayed by any attempts to claim ignorance or duress. You will answer any and all questions to the fullest of your ability and the best of your knowledge. Subsequent discovery of failure on your part to disclose any related pertinent evidence will be considered an act of sedition or sabotage."

I looked across the room towards Wightman, who looked back and gave me a slight shrug. Everyone else was watching D'Angelo and Vine.

I broke the silence. "I have a question."

Colonel D'Angelo started to turn towards me, but stopped, as though he'd concluded that I wasn't worth the effort. "If that prisoner speaks again, I'll consider it to be a deliberate attempt to hinder this investigation."

No one responded to that, so D'Angelo said, "You are all confined to this room until further notice."

He left, followed by all of the marines except Armando and Vine. The hiss of the closing door was followed by the unmistakeable sound of the lock engaging.

McConnach began, "So... what the *drokk* is that all—"

Armando softly but sharply said, "Room's bugged. No cameras in here, but they could be listening."

Takenaga approached Copus, and as she helped him to his feet softly asked, "Ideas?"

Standing in the centre of the room, Vine looked at all of us in turn. "The corporal is right. The colonel's people will be listening. But it doesn't matter because he's going to execute us all anyway, just as soon as he's sure you haven't spoken to anyone else."

Wightman asked, "Why? What does he think we've *done*?"

Corporal Armando said, "You know about me. That's all. You know I exist." He looked down at his cuffed hands. "I'm proof of the project's failure."

Vine nodded. "The purpose of Huygens Base is to build a better soldier. It has to be done out here, far from the reach of anyone on Earth. Covert factors from Mega-City One, Mega-City Two and Texas-City working together... it's more than enough to have the Sov-Blocks and every other city worried." She turned to me. "A lot of the work was inspired by you, Dredd."

I said, "I'm far from the first prisoner to have his body modified."

"That's not what I'm talking about. A long time ago Morton Judd put into action his plans to build better Judges. You and your brother were the success that inspired Colonel D'Angelo to do the same with the marines. There's a facility on Oberon that's growing clone embryos from heavily-tweaked DNA. I've seen what they have so far..." She barely suppressed a shudder. "The results are not promising. They're a long way from success. That's why D'Angelo has turned to body-modification instead. Again, inspired by you."

"How so?"

"Captain Harrow's reports mentioned discovering you out in the Bronze, almost dead. She wrote that if you and... Guildford, was it? ...If you'd swapped places, you would almost certainly have survived long enough to make it back to the prison on foot."

Wightman said, "Wait, stop! For Grud's sake, the more she tells us, the more likely it is that the Colonel will want to execute us!"

"That's inevitable," Armando said. "I know this is worth nothing, but I'm sorry. It was *my* malfunction that sparked this. Everyone in this room will die and D'Angelo will craft a credible reason. He has almost limitless resources and he'll do anything to prevent his superiors from learning the truth."

McConnach asked, "How long do we have?"

Vine said, "As soon as he's certain that we didn't make contact with the prison, that's it. He'll give the order."

I knew that it was time to make some sort of move, but exactly what I *could* do, I wasn't sure. So I said, "That could be bad... if he suspects that one of us *did* talk to someone at the prison, then he might just decide to wipe them out too." As I spoke I turned in a slow circle, examining the room. No windows, and the only way in was the doors through which we'd entered.

"Except of course that until a couple of minutes ago, all we knew was that this was a base, not what it was for. That's on *you*, Vine." I looked at Takenaga, put one finger to my lips and beckoned her forward. "And you too, Armando. If you hadn't lost control... But why don't you do that again? Go berserk and break us out of here?"

Takenaga stopped in front of me wearing a puzzled expression. I gestured that I wanted the pen in her pocket, and she reluctantly handed it over.

I crouched down and snapped the pen in two, still speaking: "But you can't, can you? Something triggered that, some part of the experiment. *That's* what he's covering up. Not that you're a failure, because clearly you're *not*. You're rational and in control." I popped out the pen's ink capsule and used the edge of the lid to prise the stopper from the capsule. "But still. You took down over thirty of your fellow soldiers without getting so much as a scratch and there's no way *all* of them were caught unaware." I put the pen's nib flat on the floor under my heel, then slowly rocked back until I heard a tiny *crack*.

Inside was a circuit board half the size of a fingernail clipping that held the tiniest lithium battery in common use, not much bigger than a grain of salt. "Some of them had to have heard the gunfire, right?"

Not a lot of people knew that everything they wrote with their handy, disposable ball-point pen was logged in the pen's memory circuits, and there was a reason for that: if they did, they'd stop using those pens. There've been a number of cases where the evidence provided by such pens has proven vital. Not *many* cases, but even one perp caught is worth it. So the people don't know that their pens are logging their words, and they'll never find out, because Judges are rarely required to reveal the source of their evidence.

By now, everyone was crowded around me, but I tried not to let that distract me. This was tricky enough as it was, let alone having to do it while keeping up a running diatribe to distract whoever might be listening.

"Still, I'm betting that Colonel D'Angelo isn't too pleased that his prototype super-soldier was beaten by a former Judge who hasn't been on the streets in years." I pulled the battery away from the board, then motioned for everyone but Armando to step back.

"He's not going to take that lying down." As I said that, I gestured for Armando to sit down next to me.

He looked puzzled, but curious, and did as I suggested. I made a circular motion with my index finger to indicate that he should roll onto his side, and when he did, I lay down almost flat on my stomach with my face close to the handcuffs on his wrists.

The pen's ink capsule contained about eight drops. Just about enough.

I'd never done this before, and certainly hadn't ever expected to do it in full view of sub-warden Copus, but we weren't left with a lot of choice. "Maybe he should have just recruited *Judges*, right? Let the Academy of Law train his troops for him and then pick the best. If he'd come to me after I graduated, I would have said yes."

Each set of cuffs had an electronic lock that responded to a coded—and uncrackable—signal from its corresponding key. But every electronic device needs a source of power, and in the cuffs that was a battery attached to the internal lock, the whole thing shielded in the cuffs' tough titanium-polymer shell. But batteries run down and have to be replaced or recharged; the polymer shell couldn't be permanently sealed.

Holding Armando's arms steady with one hand, I dripped some

ink from Takenaga's pen onto the underside of the cuffs, at the seam, all around the tightly-fitting battery cover.

I silently counted the seconds while some of the ink filtered its way down into the cuffs, then at the six-second mark I dropped the pen's tiny lithium battery onto the ink.

The ink is marketed as safe—absolutely non-toxic, non-corrosive—and that's true. But it *is* highly conductive. The ink seeped into the cuffs' battery compartment, short-circuiting and discharging the battery. That shuts down the cuffs completely; a safety measure in case the prisoners attempt to break them open.

But the cuffs' circuitry is smart enough to know that the battery will have to be recharged at some point, and it can't be recharged if the prisoner is still *wearing* the cuffs: you don't let the prisoners have access to the charger. So to make sure that happens, if the circuitry detects only the tiniest trickle of power, it'll register that as an *almost*-discharged battery and use that last burst of power to open the lock.

Corporal Armando's cuffs went *click*, and fell open.

I stepped back, and everyone else in the room was staring at me.

Have to tell you, having my mouth sealed up was the only thing that kept me from grinning like an idiot.

Twelve

I TOLD THE others, "No need to be silent. We should talk to each other. If D'Angelo's people *are* listening in, let them hear five different conversations. That'll keep them busy."

The others began to speak, awkwardly at first, but with growing confidence—and growing volume.

Leaning close and speaking so low that even someone standing a metre away wouldn't have heard, I asked Vine, "If we can get past the doors, how do we get out of the base?"

I'd realised something on the way in from the bus. We were entering the base via the blast-hole in the wall; but clearly there had to be other entrances. D'Angelo hadn't wanted us to use one because then we'd know where they were.

But Vine and Armando already knew.

She told me, "We're twenty metres underground now. All the useable exits are on the top level."

"And getting to them means going through the colonel's people... okay." I had to think about this. Our assets were meagre, to say the least. Of the guards, only Copus and Takenaga were—in my opinion—in fighting shape, and Copus was currently incapacitated, courtesy the bullet in his shoulder. Sloane moved at the speed of a tortoise trudging through tar, and McConnach was long past her prime. Of my fellow prisoners, only Zera Kurya would be of much use. Kellan Wightman had lost his edge. He would never have admitted it, and certainly worked hard to maintain the illusion that he was still a hard-as-depleted-uranium-nails Judge, but I could see the truth. Titan had broken him, as it had so many others.

Sloane tapped me on the shoulder and pointed towards Copus, who was now sitting against a side wall with the torn-off sleeve of his jacket wrapped around the wound in his arm.

I squatted next to him and he leaned forward a little so that he could whisper in my ear. "That was some trick with the cuffs, Rico. How long have you been sitting on that one?"

"Since long before my arrest."

"Heh. Well, I *know* you have a way out of this, don't you? Do what it takes to get us out. Don't let me down."

"I have some ideas, but mostly they begin with me being on the other side of those doors." I signalled to Vine, and when she was close enough, I asked, "How many marines does the colonel have in his guard? Judging by the size of his ship, it's not more than ten."

"Eleven. And it's safe guess they're all here—he never travels without all of them."

Copus asked, "But who's pulling *his* strings?"

"Unknown."

"Okay... If we can somehow take him down, what sort of retaliation can we expect?"

Again, Vine shrugged. "The project is black ops, so only a handful of people back home will know about it."

I said, "Then we need to take the colonel alive, because *he'll* know who his bosses are."

Everyone stopped talking almost at once, and I realised that they were all looking at the door.

The marine called Sears was entering through the doorway, followed by two of his colleagues. Sears stopped two steps in, and his men took up positions on either side of him. "Colonel D'Angelo has reached a decision. There has been a tragic accident and your transport never returned. Governor Dodge will be informed of the truth to encourage his silence. You..." He stopped, staring at Armando, then glanced at the soldier beside him. "Ordered you to search and scan them for *keys*, Malaki."

"Yes, sir. We did. Clean sweep."

"Then how the hell is Armando out of his cuffs? Put fresh ones on him and bring him. He's the sole survivor of Huygens Base."

The colonel wasn't the only one who had reached a decision.

I had never been the most popular of prisoners, but this was going to relegate me to the bottom of everyone's party list.

But, hey, sometimes you have to grow a pair and make the hard choices.

That's what being a Judge is all about. The hard choices. A perp attacks a citizen, hits him with a fire-axe, for example. So you come on the scene. What do you do? Chase down the perp and leave the wounded cit to bleed out, or tend to the cit in the hope that you *might* get a chance to track down the perp before he kills again? You can't do both. Pick one. And pick *fast*, because that cit is dying and the perp is fleeing.

Every day at the academy we were posed questions like that. Every day from the age of five.

There are few easy or obvious answers to those moral dilemmas. They're rarely clear-cut. A Judge learns to quickly and instinctively weigh up all the options, to make the choice that will lead to the best possible outcome. We don't always get it right—we're only human—but doing nothing is *also* a choice. How do you want to spend the rest of your life? "Damn it, if only I'd done *something*!" or "Damn it, I wish I'd done that *other* thing!"

So you act, because inaction is death, if not of the body, then of the soul.

I chose to act. I weighed up the options and the possibilities and the risks, and even as Sears was saying the words "Governor Dodge will be informed of the truth," I was starting to move.

Four steps to the left, keeping watch on the marines. I couldn't see their eyes behind those opaque faceplates, but I could read their body language: soldiers are trained to point their guns at the most obvious and immediate threat. Even when they're officially not targeting someone, their guns will have a bias in that direction.

All three of them had their weapons angled towards Armando. Understandable, because as far as they were concerned, Armando was the most dangerous person in the room. They clearly weren't taking into account that the only reason he was in the room was because someone had captured him. A wise soldier should conclude that maybe the captor was a bigger threat than the captive.

My step put me directly behind Kellan Wightman. His impressive height and build almost completely hid me from the marines' view, and his mass was vital for my plan.

I grabbed the back of his collar with my left hand, and his waistband with my right, and pushed hard.

I'm not as strong as some prisoners, but I'm no shrimp. I pushed Wightman hard enough and fast enough that he didn't even have time to react as he stumbled forward towards the marines.

They took half a second to realise what was happening: a large prisoner was rushing at them.

Another half-second to swing their guns in his direction.

But that was all I needed.

I pushed Wightman and dropped, ducked down to the side.

The marines opened fire and their automatic weapons ripped twin tracks of five-millimetre rounds across his body.

I hit the ground and lunged forward, crashing into the legs of the marine on Sears' right.

The marine went down, his gun still spraying the room—but I couldn't let myself think about that. We both crashed to the floor and I reached up and snatched the handgun from Sears' belt. Their armour was bullet-proof, I knew that, but at this range even a handgun could get through, if it hit the right spot: the elbow and knee joints... and directly under the helmet.

Two shots into the underside of the marine's jaw and the inside of his visor was red.

But Sears was no slacker. He swung his automatic at me and would certainly have blown me away if Corporal Vine hadn't slammed into the third marine—Malaki—knocking him against Sears. I swear I felt one of Sears' rounds skim across my back.

Vine ripped Malaki's gun from his hands, but Sears was recovering, swearing as he again tried to aim.

That was when Zera Kurya lunged at him and headbutted him square in the faceplate—that *had* to hurt—hard enough to knock him back out into the corridor.

I still had Sears' pistol: two point-blank shots to Malaki's right knee and he was down, screaming.

Then he slid *into* the room and I turned to see Corporal Armando dragging him in by the foot. "Get Sears!" Armando barked.

Kurya threw herself after him, using my back as a springboard, and again crashed into Sears, slamming him against the far wall.

I'd never seen Zera Kurya in action. I'd heard about her hand-to-hand skills, of course, but to actually watch her fighting was a unique experience.

Sears had fifteen, maybe twenty, kilogrammes on her, was wearing full body armour and was armed. She had her fists.

Her first punch cracked his helmet's visor and knocked his head back. The second punch was aimed at his throat, and snapped his head forward again.

A knee to the midriff, then she grabbed his right arm and hoisted him over her shoulder, slamming him face-first into the ground.

She pulled the rifle from his grip, jammed the muzzle under the backplate of Sears' armour and emptied the clip.

By the time she straightened up, blood was seeping from every joint in his armour.

Next to me, Vine was staring in shock. I could see she knew we'd done the right thing, but Sears and the others had been her colleagues, of a sort, and she'd already lost thirty-four others that day.

"They're going to kill us for this," she said to Armando. "At the very least."

I said, "They won't. They'll never find out."

On Copus's instructions, Sloane and McConnach started to remove the marines' armour and take their weapons. That was when I realised that Malaki was dead too.

I'd only shot him in the knee. Armando had broken his neck, barehanded.

But still, the others were looking at me as though *I* were the monster, rather than the man who'd just saved them.

Vine had Malaki's assault rifle aimed at my face. "Hand over the gun, Dredd."

"Not a chance. I just *saved* all of your—"

Armando snatched the gun from my hand before I even noticed him starting to move.

Takenaga said, "Jovus, Rico... Wightman."

I said, "What? It had to be done. They would have killed *all* of us."

"You used him as a decoy."

I nodded. "I know. And if I hadn't, we'd *all* be dead. Wightman was going to die anyway." I didn't see the problem. "You know why he was here, don't you? He was an arsonist. Put the lives of millions of cits at risk in Mega-City Two. Four of them died. And he was absolutely unrepentant. *You* know that, Takenaga—you ran his counselling sessions!"

Sloane said, "He was your *friend.*"

I turned to him. "Doesn't change anything. Wightman was scum among scum and you know that. *Everyone* knows that. *He* knew it. The only reason he wasn't executed when they caught him was because they need strong drokkers like him in this place. Now, thanks to him, we've got a chance that we didn't have before." I looked down at Wightman's mangled body. "There was no way we were all going to get out of this alive. So well done, Kellan. You became a hero at the last minute, even if you didn't know you were going to do it."

I stepped back, away from the still-spreading pool of Kellan Wightman's blood, and looked around at the others. "Are we going to spend the rest of the day debating the moral issues here, or are we going to deal with the actual threat?"

Copus glanced around the room. "Three down. So that's eight left, plus D'Angelo. Pity their armour is custom-made. Okay... Takenaga and Sloane, you'll stay here, guard Kurya and Dredd. Lock the room behind us."

I put my hand out to stop him. "No. You don't have the skills or the experience for this. We need to move fast and you're wounded. It should be me, Takenaga, Kurya, Armando and Vine. Sloane and McConnach are too slow and too soft."

McConnach said, "Mister Copus, we can't give guns to *prisoners!* Seriously, that's insane! Look what this drokker just did to his best friend!"

Copus stared at me through narrowed but unblinking eyes for a moment. "They're not *getting* guns. But Rico Dredd has got a will to live that dwarfs any of ours—that's what's going to get him out of this. And we don't have time to argue. You do this *right*, Dredd. Do we have an understanding?"

"You can count on me, boss. You *know* that. I—"

"Shut up. We're not friends." He turned to Takenaga, and jabbed an index finger at me. "This drokker gives you *any* reason to doubt him—any reason at all—shoot him in the head. *You're* in command here, Kalai. Not him."

Takenaga nodded. "Acknowledged."

Vine handed a communicator to Copus and tossed one of the marines' rifles to Takenaga. "The walls dampen the gunfire but they'll be expected to check in soon. We need to move."

Thirteen

Vine and Armando led the way, rapidly swapping positions as they made their way along the steel-walled corridor, checking each room as they passed.

Takenaga followed, her bottom lip firmly clamped between her teeth and sweat on her forehead. I didn't know much about her background before she left Hondo City, but I'd always assumed she'd been a Judge. Right now, I wasn't so sure about that. She did *not* look comfortable. She was holding the assault rifle like it was poisonous.

Kurya and I held back. We'd each had similar training to the marines, but this was their territory, not ours, and we were unarmed. I intended to rectify that at the earliest possible opportunity, even though—as we'd already learned—a standard assault weapon wasn't effective against the marines' armour at much more than a metre.

Ahead, Armando silently signalled the all-clear, and he and Vine moved on.

Kurya gestured for me to go ahead.

I said, "No, you next."

She shook her head. "You still have Wightman's blood on you. Literally. I do not trust you."

"I'm unarmed," I said as I moved on.

"A weapon is not required for strangulation."

"Paranoid," I muttered. Then, over my shoulder, I added, "I had no choice, Zera. They were about to kill *all* of us. You'd have done the same thing."

"I would not. You betrayed a fellow prisoner, Rico. If we survive this and return to the prison, you will have a target on your forehead like you have never known. You'll be dead in a day."

"I don't care," I said. "I made the only logical choice."

"You could have picked one of the *guards!*" I'd never heard Kurya so close to losing her temper.

Takenaga turned back and glared at us, mouthing the words, "Shut up!"

We resumed following them.

Kurya was right. I could have chosen a guard. Sloane was the obvious choice, except that while he wasn't the only one who knew how to drive the bus—I could have driven it myself—no one else knew the way back to the prison.

The next obvious choice was Copus, but the position was all wrong: he'd been sitting with his back to the wall. No way to get behind him.

And Takenaga and McConnach were out for reasons of bulk, or lack thereof. It's hard to hide behind someone smaller than you.

So, yes, Kellan Wightman had died and that was sad on some levels; I'm sure that in most cases he would have had my back. But let's not forget that he was an arsonist, and guilty of manslaughter. Not to mention a racist: he despised the Fornies—the Californian Secessionists—with a fervour usually reserved for the sort of preacher you see on Sunday morning TV broadcasting from a mega-church.

He was not a nice guy, that's what I'm saying.

And it was also true that when, or *if*, we got back to the prison, word would get out about what I'd done, and my life would be a living hell. Every prisoner in the place was going to be out for my blood.

Except, of course, that I was now the only person who knew where Wightman had stashed his barrels of booze. Alcohol can be a great bargaining chip if used wisely.

Vine was crouched next to an open doorway, with Takenaga right behind her and Armando pressed flat against the opposite wall, his gun raised. Vine beckoned me closer, then whispered, "Corridor leads to the port stairwell... They're waiting for us."

"You're certain?"

"Heard the crackle of a radio."

"Armando should hang back. I'm guessing that he's the only reason they haven't rushed us. Without him, the colonel's entire project is a failure."

Then a man's voice, far too close for comfort, said, "You got that right, Dredd."

Vine's eyes widened, as I'm sure mine did too.

The voice was coming from the other side of the doorway, no more than a few centimetres away. If the wall hadn't been there, we'd have been leaning against each other.

Armando called out, "Who are you?"

"Lancaster. I've assumed command. I'm guessing that Sears, Malaki and Pohle are out of commission."

I said, "If you mean 'dead,' then yes."

"Sears was dumb to forget that the prisoners are former Judges," Lancaster said.

Vine said, "We have a situation here that can only end with all of your people dead, or all of ours. There's no middle ground."

"It would seem so. Vine, this facility has already been compromised. If we have to, we'll pull the plug on everything. We'll write off Armando. Colonel D'Angelo's not happy about that idea, but he understands. We've already lost so much. The sunk-cost fallacy can't continue indefinitely. Sooner or later, you've got to admit defeat. He's approaching that point now."

I said, "You don't have to do this, Lancaster."

"In the marines we're trained to follow orders without asking questions."

"In the Department of Justice we were trained to *always* ask questions."

"Is that so? Look where that's gotten you."

Armando said, "So I surrender to you, and you kill everyone here, or we continue to hold out and you kill us all anyway."

"Oh, it's—" Lancaster stopped, and we all heard footsteps approaching. "He's here."

We held our breath for a few seconds, then heard Colonel D'Angelo say, "Enough. I don't *want* to do this, but..." Something clicked on the other side, and the door silently and smoothly slid closed.

Most of the door was thick synthiglass, certainly bulletproof. The colonel now stood behind it, looking in at us.

"Door's locked from this side. Former First Lieutenant Vine knows this base. She'll confirm that there is no other way for you to reach us."

We all stood up, and he peered at us one by one, finishing with Armando. "You killed thirty-four people this morning, corporal. Thirty-four of your own colleagues."

Armando took a step closer to the door. "You're the one who turned me into a weapon."

"Perhaps. But I'm not the one who pulled the trigger. *You* did that."

I said, "So we have a stalemate."

Colonel D'Angelo smiled. "Not really, Dredd. It's not stalemate when one player holds all the cards."

"Cards? I was talking about chess. What the hell sort of game *you* playing?" I asked. I was standing beside and a little behind Takenaga, and she really was focussed on the colonel. "Whatever. Here's my move." Looking back now, it was shockingly easy to pull the gun from Takenaga's grip and press its muzzle against the back of Armando's neck.

He jumped, as did everyone else except for the colonel.

"You let us go or your experiment here is over forever."

"And when he's dead, so are you."

"Right," I said. "Now, that's what I mean by a stalemate. Neither of us can make a move."

"Unless we change the rules."

I nodded. "Now you're getting it."

"No, you're the one who's not getting it." D'Angelo stepped to the side a little to get a better view of the corporal. "You don't know *why* you went into a frenzy this morning, do you, Armando?

You don't know what it was that set you off." Colonel D'Angelo took a long, deep breath and let it out slowly, and it seemed to me that he was coming to a decision about something.

And then he said, "Doctor Riahi didn't only modify your skin, soldier. She reprogrammed the primitive centres of your brain with something she called the Berserker Protocol. You automatically respond to two key phrases. One to activate the protocol, the other to dismiss it. Only Riahi and I knew those phrases."

"That's what happened? *She* triggered the frenzy?"

D'Angelo said, "She did. The CCTV footage of the attack is of low quality, so there's no way to be certain, but I believe that Riahi wasn't awake at the time. She was talking in her sleep."

Armando swayed, and looked as though he was about to collapse. "No. No, that's not true."

"It *is*," the colonel said. "You're not a man anymore, Armando, you're a weapon. You said it yourself. You're a weapon, and you were triggered by accident." He shrugged. "A misfire. Another failure of the design team. Or another lesson learned, if you prefer. But I do still want to bring you in. It'll be difficult without Riahi's expertise, but we will attempt to adjust your programming so that it won't happen again. At least, not so easily."

Vine called out, "If you can do that, then you can probably *remove* the programming too."

D'Angelo nodded. "That's possible, but not what we want. Corporal Armando, we didn't spend billions of credits just to end up with a man who *used* to be an unstoppable killer. You understand that, don't you? Now, you will kill First Lieutenant Vine and your new friends here. And then we can clean up the last traces of this mess."

"I won't—"

D'Angelo said, "Unfettered Hematophagy."

I realised what the colonel was doing even before he had finished speaking the trigger-phrase.

My gun was still pressed against the back of Corporal John Armando's head. I pulled the trigger.

I was still too late.

Fourteen

ARMANDO DODGED THE bullet. At point-blank range. It sounds impossible, I know, but trust me: I was there.

I had the muzzle of my gun pressed against the back of his neck, at the base of his skull, and as I squeezed the trigger he moved to the left, spinning at the same time, flicking his left arm up.

By the time the round exited the barrel, Armando had both moved out of its path and knocked my arm with his left elbow.

As the bullet ricocheted off the wall next to the door, Armando jabbed the heel of his right hand into my sternum, and pulled the gun from my grip with his left hand. And I thought *I'd* been slick, when I'd grabbed the gun from Takenaga.

I crashed back into the wall behind me, but I wasn't winded or wounded—I wasn't out of the fight yet.

In the second or so it took me to recover, Armando had already disarmed Vine and was slamming my gun into Takenaga's stomach.

Armando tossed both guns aside, grabbed hold of Kurya's arm and was pulling her around, putting her between himself and me. Clearly, in this berserker state, he either didn't remember what had happened with Wightman or he didn't care. A sharp, hard punch to Kurya's face disoriented her, allowing him to manipulate her almost as though she were a plastic mannequin.

I had beaten him before, yes, but that had only been a few hours earlier. I was still aching from that fight, and I wasn't sure that I could do it again.

I could have made a grab for one of the guns, and I might have even reached it, but the angles, the positions... If I opened fire I'd hit Kurya for sure, possibly also Takenaga and Vine. I didn't want that.

Vine slammed her fist into Armando's right side with enough force to put a normal person out for good, but he barely registered it. Instead, he continued swinging Kurya around, shoving her against Vine.

I took a quick glance through the glass door: Colonel D'Angelo was staring back, watching the scene with a cold detachment. It seemed to me that he was studying Armando the same way an entomologist might study a pair of clashing insects.

But this wasn't the time for me to start studying *him*. I needed a plan.

I couldn't risk shooting Kurya, Vine or Takenaga; they were all accomplished fighters, and while they were no match for Armando, they *were* slowing him down.

He would kill them, I was certain, but right now, they were still getting in his way.

Often, the wise warrior knows he has to choose a path that his opponent won't expect. Armando—or whatever part of his brain was in control—knew I'd beaten him before, and expected me to try again. So I'd do something else.

Instead of diving for a gun, I rushed at him, reached past Kurya and slammed my fist into Armando's already-broken clavicle.

He didn't scream, but there was no mistaking the pain registering on his face.

He shoved Kurya aside and advanced on me, half staggering, clutching his shoulder. I knew I had one more shot: a quick side-kick aimed at his stomach. He instinctively dropped his hand to block the kick... That was when I added a last-second flick to my ankle that took some power out of the kick but shifted its aim.

I heard the broken halves of his clavicle crunch under my boot.

Then I ran.

Not because I was scared—I could probably take Armando in a one-on-one fight, especially now—but because the risk to the others was too high. I wanted him to abandon them completely and chase me. After all, I was clearly the bigger threat.

Some of them don't see it that way: they argue that I fled the scene. That's obviously stomm. I had the upper hand. I wasn't running from Armando, I was *leading* him. But I don't care what anyone else chooses to believe. Their opinions are considerably less important than the truth.

And my plan worked, too. I ran in the opposite direction of the gymnasium, and within seconds I could hear Armando scrabbling after me.

I have to admit, at this stage I was seriously regretting cracking his handcuffs.

The biggest disadvantage I had was that I didn't know the base, or certainly not as well as Armando did. This had been his home for seventeen months. He would have been able to move around it blindfolded and not bump into anything.

Ahead, the corridor curved to the right, and against one wall was a long red-and-pink smear—the still-drying blood and brain matter of one of the corporal's dead colleagues. After about four metres the smear dropped down to the floor and led to a thick pool of almost-congealed blood: I could feel it stick to my boots and was all too aware that I was leaving a very easy trail for Armando to follow.

But there was no sign of the body. My guess was that the colonel's men had been cleaning up.

I skidded to a stop at a junction and turned right. A trail of blood-dots on the ground disappeared under a closed door. I couldn't tell whether that meant that a body had been carried into the room or out of it; I was hoping it would turn out to be the latter.

I could still hear him behind me—any second now he'd reach the junction—but I tried the door anyway: locked. I moved on, all too aware that every door I tried would almost certainly be the same.

But a Judge doesn't quit just because the odds are against him. He keeps going. He *changes* the odds. He improvises a weapon, or he uses the enemy's strength against him. Or he changes the playing field. That's what I was about to do.

Armando had killed thirty-four people on this base. Colonel D'Angelo's people had done a rudimentary job of clearing up, but they hadn't had a lot of time. Certainly not enough time to dispose of thirty-four bodies. The smears and blood-drops on the floor told me that they'd just moved the bodies out of the way.

The military mind is efficient and methodical, so I knew that they'd have quickly developed a routine. Find the bodies, identify them, check them against the base's manifest, then move them somewhere. Can't have them stinking up the rest of the base. And you don't want them decaying, either, before a proper investigation can take place. You put the bodies into the morgue, if you have one. And if you don't, you still need to keep them cold.

The surface temperature on Titan rarely goes above minus one-eighty.

I thundered up a metal staircase, taking the steps three at a time. At the top I grabbed the rail and hauled on it hard, used it to quickly swing myself around, heading back along the upper level for the next staircase. Again, three at a time—but by now I could hear Armando on the stairs below.

Another thin line of blood-drops told me that I was still going in the right direction, but I was too slow. Or Armando was too fast, depending on how you look at it. I needed something to slow him down.

There was no way this base would have a morgue large enough to hold all those bodies. Colonel D'Angelo would have ordered his team to carry the stiffs outside to preserve them. And the only way out of a mostly-underground base is through airlocks on the upper levels.

D'Angelo had sealed himself and his team off from the berserk Corporal Armando, but he'd clearly not sealed the entire base.

Even if he *had* locked all the outer doors, the base had started life as a ship... Spaceships' airlocks have manual overrides in case of a ship-wide power-failure.

A third flight of stairs, and as I approached the top, Armando was five metres behind me and moving at twice my speed.

I dropped, planted my hands on the top step and kicked back with both feet.

I got lucky, I admit that. My left heel smashed into Armando's face and he stumbled backwards, his grace stripped away by his sheer fury.

He fell, but I didn't have the luxury of watching him tumble. I scrambled to my feet and kept going.

And there, to my left, I saw it: the inner door of an airlock large enough to take a family car. Piled up in front of it was the base's former crew. About two-thirds of them were in body bags, but clearly they'd exhausted the supply; around a dozen were crudely wrapped in blankets bound with electricians' tape.

At the left side of the door was a large, clearly-signposted recess, and in that recess was a solid, red-painted lever.

I made a dive for the lever and grabbed it just as Corporal Armando's hands locked around my right ankle.

I slammed the lever down, and the airlock's inner door instantly dropped down into its cavity in the floor as Armando dragged me away.

Earlier, Vine had told me that he wasn't superhuman. Now, I wasn't so sure. His powerful fingers felt like they were going to crush my ankle.

But that feeling didn't last long. In fact, I barely had time to register it before Armando—still holding on with his left hand—ploughed his right fist hard into my stomach.

The impact jerked my hand free of the lever and I crashed to the floor, but Armando still hadn't let go. He single-handedly heaved me up and swung me by my leg, bringing my face down to his rapidly-moving foot. There was nothing I could do to avoid it.

His boot hit my forehead with enough force that for a moment I thought my neck was going to snap.

Growing desperate, I flailed around with my left foot and by chance more than anything else I managed to hit him in the side of his neck with my heel. That staggered him for a second, long enough for me to get my right hand behind his left knee. I pulled, and he buckled.

I squirmed free, scrabbling my way across the floor towards the airlock. Ten metres to the second lever, the one that would open the outer door.

And Armando crashed into me again, his shoulder slamming into the small of my back. We tumbled to the floor, skidded a little further into the airlock, but now he was grabbing, punching, kicking. He slashed at my face with clawed fingers and ripped away one of the prosthetic pieces of my cybernetic breathing apparatus.

The piece had been bonded to my skin and it tore off a chunk, but, worse, I could feel the ends of tubes scraping the inside of my lungs.

There was no way I could beat him. I knew that now. Armando was too strong, too fast. And you can't reason with an enemy who's in the thrall of a berserker rage.

Then another blow slammed into my throat and I felt my voicebox pop out, heard it clatter wetly across the floor.

And I saw a possible way out.

If you can't outfight your enemy, and you can't outrun them, and you've got nothing else to hand... Purge your sinus filters right into their face.

It's a simple process, something that Wightman and I and the other mods did every day. You remove your voicebox, hit the switch on the cybernetic implant under your right ear, and whoosh. Or 'splash,' if you prefer.

Our sinus implants don't produce a *lot* of artificial snot, but it's pretty nasty stuff. Sticky, stringy, laced with dust and dirt and sand and specks of blood.

I triggered mine and it gushed out, hit Corporal John Armando square in the face.

He flinched, squirmed away to try and clean it.

And I jumped up and grabbed the outer door's manual lever.

If we'd been in space, the air would have been blown out of the base, but on the surface of Titan the air pressure is actually greater than that on Earth—and in the base—so instead, Titan's atmosphere rushed *in*.

I'd planned for that, of course. It wasn't the air pressure that I'd needed. It was the cold.

I had to cover up the hole in my throat while I raced after my voicebox, but that only took a few seconds.

And in those few seconds, Corporal Armando collapsed shuddering to the floor and passed out. His polymer-laced skin shielded him from the cold, but his lungs were still human: ice forming inside your lungs is not a nice feeling.

I closed the airlock door again, gave Armando a few hard kicks just to be sure he wasn't faking, then allowed myself a minute to sit down and rest. I mean, it had been a long day. And it wasn't over.

Fifteen

"I'll make a deal with you, Colonel," I said into the communicator. I'd found it in a vest pocket on one of the corpses, along with four other communicators, a hand-held computer that I was sure would come in useful back at the prison, a deck of playing cards, fourteen packs of gum—again, great currency among the prisoners—and three hundred and eighty-three credits in cash. Which is, of course, the best currency of all.

No guns, knives or any other weapons, unfortunately.

There was probably a lot more to find on the rest of the bodies, but I didn't have time.

Colonel D'Angelo said, "I don't think you're in a position to negotiate, Dredd."

"Actually, I am." I was walking back through the base. Not running: I was still hopeful of spotting something that might be worth smuggling back.

After I'd resealed the airlock doors—having had a brief look outside to see where I was in relation to the artificial plateau—finding the communicators had been my first priority.

The marines had guns and armour and a small but powerful ship, and I was sure that one of their last acts would be to destroy the base. Or maybe just power up its engines and fly it away. Land it elsewhere on Titan, or any one of Saturn's other moons.

"Corporal Armando is still alive, you'll be pleased to hear. He might not be the super-soldier you were trying to create, given I beat him twice, but then I was an exceptional Judge."

"And what is this deal that you believe is worth my time listening to?"

I descended the second flight of stairs. "You take Armando and leave us alone. Simple as that. We're not going to tell anyone what happened here, because you're going to allow us to raid the base's stores. I know you've got better food than we do. That food will buy our silence."

There was no response, just static, and I was about to repeat myself when D'Angelo finally asked, "You expect me to believe that?"

"Have you ever been to prison, Colonel? We know—we *all* know—that there's no way off this rock before our sentence is done. We hate that, but we accept it. Now we have smaller ambitions, and one of them is nicer food. It's the little luxuries that keep us going."

"Where is Corporal Armando, Dredd?"

By now, I'd reached the curved corridor with the blood-smear on the wall, which allayed my slight worry that I'd gotten lost. "You'll never find him before he suffocates. But you let us all go back to our transport, and I'll tell you exactly where he is."

The corridor straightened out, and I saw Vine, Takenaga and Kurya on the floor. There was no way to tell from here whether they were alive, but I was sure they must be. There had barely been fifteen seconds between when I started running and when I heard Armando following me: surely not enough time to kill three people barehanded.

I slowed as I approached Vine, and if I'd still been in possession of my original lungs, I'm sure I'd have been holding my breath.

Her fingers were twitching. She was alive.

Takenaga, too, was clearly still with us. She was moaning softly.

Kurya was further way, beyond the synthiglass door.

I neared the door, where I could see the Colonel's shadow. I stopped walking and softly asked, "You still there?"

"I'm here. I'm considering your offer." A few silent seconds drifted past. "Dredd, you have no way of knowing that I won't just kill you once I have Armando back."

"I know that." I stepped out in front of the door, and D'Angelo jumped back: he'd not been expecting me. "How old are you, Colonel?"

He lowered the communicator and frowned at me. "Why is that relevant?"

"You seem young for an officer of your rank. And you've never been in combat. I can tell by the way you move. So what is it? You were fast-tracked to this position because you're some kind of military genius? Something like that?"

He gave me a slight smile. "It's exactly like that. I'm twenty-two. Recruited out of elementary school. Apparently I have the ideal combination of a very high IQ, vivid imagination and no moral compass. I am what you would call a high-functioning sociopath."

I stepped closer to the door. "Yeah. Me too. So where are we now, D'Angelo? Where do we stand on our deal?"

"You'd be a fool to trust me, Dredd. And I know you're not a fool. Nor am I. What's your angle?"

"No angle. I know we won't come out of this alive unless you permit that. I was a Judge, we understand these things. Sometimes all you can hope for is a chance to walk away." I glanced down at Zera Kurya. I still couldn't tell whether she was alive or dead. "But I can sweeten the deal a little. You'll like this, trust me."

He shook his head. "There's nothing you can offer me that—"

"I beat your super-soldier. Twice. He's stronger and faster and considerably more experienced than I am, and I beat him." I put my index finger on one of the scratches on my face, then pressed it against the glass, leaving a bloody fingerprint. "Here's my offer. My DNA. I'm a first-generation clone of Eustace Fargo, the first Chief Judge of Mega-City One. You want to find the ultimate super-soldier, an unbeatable living weapon?" I smiled. "Colonel, you're *looking* at him."

THE HANDOVER WAS awkward. Tense as a twelve-string guitar about to get married on a tightrope.

All of the Colonel's people, all of mine, at the same time.

We met at the halfway point between the big bus and the blast-hole in the side of the fake plateau. And we all kept our promises. No weapons, no tricks.

Sloane and McConnach helped carry Kurya into the bus—she still hadn't regained consciousness, but at least she was alive—then we loaded up eleven crates of supplies hastily plundered from the base's stores. Once that was done, one by one the others climbed on board, including First Lieutenant Vine, until it was only me and Copus standing in front of Colonel D'Angelo and his marines. The colonel's faceplate was transparent, so I knew it was him. I still had no idea what Lancaster or any of the others looked like.

"So where is he?" Lancaster asked.

"Not yet," I said. "We *all* have to be on the bus."

The colonel nodded. "I remember. But, Dredd, we've got your DNA now. Why do we still need Armando?"

Sub-warden Copus asked, "How *much* did you spend creating him?"

D'Angelo smiled. "Too much to write off. I'll keep my word, Dredd. You just be sure you keep yours. If word of this place gets out, we'll wipe your prison off the face of Titan. You'll be atomised long before anyone on Earth knows what's happened."

"We'd gain nothing from ratting on you. It's not like we have any leverage."

Behind me, Copus climbed onto the bus and passed through the airlock cycle, then it was my turn. I climbed up and then turned back to give the marines a final nod.

"Top level," I said. "Inside the big airlock. I put the corporal in one of the body bags. You're going to need everyone to dig him out."

Lancaster laughed, then turned away, gesturing to his team to run ahead.

But the Colonel hesitated. "I could get you *out*, Dredd. I know people who have Chief Judge Goodman's ear. You agree to serve the remainder of your sentence working for me and you'll have a much better quality of life."

"Let's just get this deal out of the way first," I said. I gave him a wave, then closed the outer airlock door.

Before the inner door was even open, I shouted to Sloane, "We need to go—now!"

Sloane said, "What?" but he was already firing up the engine.

Copus shoved the door open the rest of the way, and grabbed hold of my collar. "What the hell have you *done*, Rico?"

I forced myself to keep calm. "He tried to kill us. I don't make deals with people who've tried to kill me."

There was no guarantee that it would work; I knew that. But the chances were strong. I might not be as academically gifted as Colonel Peter D'Angelo, but *he* had never worked the streets of Mega-City One.

A lack of conscience was no match for knowing how to fight dirty.

About four minutes into the journey, I pulled my communicator out of my pocket, set it down and jacked up the volume for everyone to hear.

A muffled voice said, "He was lying! Why would he hide Armando in a body bag?"

Another voice: "So we wouldn't see him so easily. That's what hiding something *means*, spugwit!"

Rustling sounds, then a third voice, clearer: "Sergeant Lancaster—something under there! That one is moving!"

I could picture the scene: Lancaster and the others checking through the body bags they'd piled up earlier. It would take them a few minutes to free Armando from underneath his former colleagues. Probably a lot less time than it had taken me to pile their bodies on top of him.

Lancaster: "Get him out of there. You two, keep your weapons ready. And a set of cuffs."

More grunting and thumping as bodies were pulled from the heap, then the first voice again, much clearer now: "Cut him out, Evans."

A knife slicing through thick plastic. I turned to the others in the bus. "Don't worry. I tied him up."

Then Lancaster again: "What...? Oh, right. Dredd put a helmet on him so he could breathe under there. Smart. Okay. Get him on his feet. But leave the tape on his mouth and his hands tied."

Colonel D'Angelo, sounding several metres away. "He's alive. So Dredd wasn't lying."

"No, sir," Lancaster said. "What's our next move?"

"Take Evans and get back to the ship. Destroy the prison transport before it can make contact."

Copus muttered, "Stomm!" then turned to Sloane. "Full speed! We can't outrun it but—"

I laughed. "No need, boss." I picked up the communicator and hit the *Transmit* stud. "Hey, Colonel, you back-stabbing drokker!"

A second's silence, then Lancaster's voice, very clear. "There's a communicator in the helmet—they've been listening!"

"We have," I said. "And now it's *your* turn to listen. All of you. Including Corporal John Armando." I took a deep breath, savouring the moment. "Unfettered Hematophagy."

Their screams were loud, but didn't last very long.

After some debate, Copus ordered Sloane to turn around, taking us back to the base once more.

By the time we got in, Armando had reverted to the same comatose state he'd been in when I first saw him, and, well, I won't say it was *easy* to subdue him again, but between us we managed it.

HUYGENS BASE IS still there, to the best of my knowledge. One day someone will find it, and maybe they'll wonder where it came from and why there are so many corpses on board. They might even wonder why there's a small, unmarked military-grade ship in the hangar.

If anyone does ever start asking questions, none of us who survived that rescue mission will talk, I know that for sure.

Corporal John Armando and First Lieutenant Salome Vine were picked up several months later by the next ship from Earth. We will probably never know what happened to them after that.

Kellan Wightman's death was listed as an accident. Unavoidable.

At least the 'unavoidable' part of that is true. I knew him. He might not have wanted to die that way, but I like to think that he would have understood.

I didn't want to do it, but it was the choice that led to the best outcome. I'm not happy with that, but I can live with it.

Just like I can live with the endless winds that howl across

Titan, rattling the windows and shaking the buildings, the newbie prisoners screaming and crying and praying and pleading, the mine's machinery that never stops rumbling and grinding. I've become acclimatised. None of that keeps me awake any more.

I can sleep at night.

The End

About the Author

Irish Author **Michael Carroll** is a former chairperson of the Irish Science Fiction Association and has previously worked as a postman and a computer programmer/systems analyst. A reader of *2000 AD* right from the very beginning, Michael is the creator of the acclaimed *Quantum Prophecy/Super Human* series of superhero novels for the Young Adult market.

His comic work includes *Judge Dredd* and *DeMarco, PI* for *2000 AD* and *Judge Dredd Megazine* (Rebellion), *Jennifer Blood* for Dynamite Entertainment and *Razorjack* for Titan Books.

www.michaelowencarroll.com

Coming soon:

RICO DREDD: THE TITAN YEARS

FOR I HAVE SINNED

Read a teaser now...

Prologue

Pastor Elvene Mandt Carbonara said, "We dwell in darkness. Our physical lives are but a brief flare, nothing more. A flicker. We were devoid of physical form for an eternity before, and will be devoid of a physical form for an eternity after. In the grand scale of the lifespan of Grud's glorious cosmos, we might as well not have lived at all."

Pastor Carbonara had been the Senior Arch-Primate of the Eighth Church of Grud the Unforgiving, a religious sect quite popular in southern Euro-Cit. She was about forty, I think. Tall with sallow skin, a wide frame but a narrow head, a noticeably asymmetrical hairline and an unsettling under-bite. Not easy on the eye.

But then neither am I, I know that. I wasn't criticising her looks, just commenting.

She'd go through months-long phases where she spoke solely in quotes from her Church's religious tracts and the rest of us were never sure whether she believed any of it, or she was just messing with us, or if it was a smokescreen for something else. That last one is most likely: she was scared, and talked non-stop to mask her fear.

She'd been on Titan for over a year but this was my first time working directly alongside her. I'd seen her many times, of course, but like most of us prisoners I kept my distance whenever possible.

One of those rules of prison life. Steer clear of the ones who talk to themselves, or flinch at the invisible fairies buzzing around them, or claim to have invented a way to turn dirt into coffee... because crazy is contagious.

So the Pastor generated an invisible force-field around herself by constantly talking about the afterlife, and that kept her reasonably safe from the psychopaths.

But it didn't keep away those who were looking for some form of guidance. The "lost souls" who seem to be destined to stand behind more eloquent people while angrily shouting, "Yeah!" and waving their fists in the air.

We were out in the Bronze, one-forty-something kilometres west of the prison complex, and the Pastor's latest diatribe had begun within minutes of sub-warden Kalai Takenaga telling her, "Carbonara, you're with Dredd. He'll show you the ropes. Dredd, go easy on her."

As we'd walked away from the bus Carbonara stared down at her feet and muttered something with each step. I'd made the mistake of asking her what she was doing.

"Blessing the footsteps. She who blesseth the steps of her feet shall forever walk upright and steady in the house of Grud. Colonials, chapter twelve, verse six. Have you been saved, Rico Dredd?"

I declined to answer, and that was when she hit me with the piece about dwelling in darkness.

I didn't want to get drawn into any kind of argument or debate. I said, "See all these loose rocks? See those two wheelbarrows? You take one of the barrows. I don't care which. If you see any rocks with a silver streak through them, or silver speckles..." I reached down and scooped up a fist-sized rock. "Like this? See? You find rocks like this, anything from the size of your thumb upwards, you put them into your barrow."

She nodded, but it was more of a bow, with her environment suit bending slightly at the hips rather than the neck. "Collect the ones with the silver. Got it. And then?"

"And then you keep going until your barrow is almost too heavy to push, and then you push it back towards the truck. The crew there will empty it for you, and then you come back here with the empty barrow and repeat the process until you run out of rocks or the sub-warden tells us it's time to quit. When we've picked this area clean, we come back with diggers and sieves. Got to get every molecule of iridium."

Pastor Carbonara looked down at her gloved hands. "These hands were designed for clasping in prayer, not picking up rocks. These are blessed hands, holy instruments of the all-strong Grud who shall—"

"I don't care how magic you think your hands are. You ordered the murders of eighty-two former members of your cult so now you get to pick up rocks. Believe me, this is one of the easiest jobs on this whole damn moon so my advice is you shut up and get to work."

She raised her head and glared at me through her suit's tinted visor. "There is a special booth in Hell's foetid diner reserved for the likes of you, Rico Dredd. The sins of the wicked are a deposit in the bank of hell, and their reward is hefty dividend of unbearable torment every day, forever. So it is written in the letter from Saint Brenda to the Pomeranians."

"Just go pick up the damn rocks!"

Sub-warden Takenaga called over to me, "Trouble, Dredd?"

"Not yet," I called back. "Any chance I can trade partners?"

"Take a guess."

Within half an hour of working alongside Pastor Carbonara I could have happily killed her. After another half-hour I would have been just as happy for her to kill me.

I had known others who talked as much. Cadet Wagner had been a chatterbox, as had Elemeno Pea, the first prisoner I got to know on Titan. But the Pastor was something else entirely. For four solid hours she methodically sorted through the rocks and scree and did a damn good job of it, I have to say, but she did not once stop talking about her church, about Grud, about sinners.

We'd been assigned a thirty-metre-square area to clear so I couldn't move far enough away to be completely out of earshot, but I noticed that the inmates working around us seemed to be keeping to the far sides of their patches.

I'd no choice but to try to tune out her rhetoric and let it wash over me.

You don't argue with a crazy Grud-botherer because they train for that. You can't fast-track to the end of their sermon by pretending to agree with them because they have an inexhaustible supply of fresh diatribes lined up and ready to go. And you certainly don't ask a religious nut, "What do you mean, exactly?" because they will tell you.

In the Academy of Law back in Mega-City One we were taught how to remain calm under pressure. A vital skill for a Judge, and handy for inmates, too. I was able to ignore Pastor Elvene Mandt Carbonara, to mentally turn her volume dial back down from eleven to about one or two and just ride it out.

But not every prisoner had that skill. Many of them had never been Judges, or they were out of practice.

Over time, some of them began to listen to what she had to say.

She was a charismatic, imaginative, intelligent, very persuasive spiritual crackpot sentenced to life on a half-frozen moon with a little over two hundred of the toughest, most dangerous people who ever walked the Earth.

Any fool should have been able to see that this was not a match made in Heaven.

18829681R00081

Printed in Great Britain
by Amazon